THE PREACHER THE POLITICIAN AND THE PLAYBOY

VANESSA MILLER

THE PREACHER
THE POLITICIAN
AND THE PLAYBOY

MORRISON FAMILY SECRETS

WHITAKER
HOUSE

THE PREACHER, THE POLITICIAN, AND THE PLAYBOY
Morrison Family Secrets ~ Book Two

A Three-in-One Collection of Novellas Featuring:
THE PREACHER (© 2011 [eBook, *The Preacher's Choice*], 2014 by Vanessa Miller)
THE POLITICIAN (© 2011 [eBook, *The Politician's Wife*], 2014 by Vanessa Miller)
THE PLAYBOY (© 2011 [eBook, *The Playboy's Redemption*], 2014 by Vanessa Miller)

Vanessa Miller
www.vanessamiller.com

ISBN: 978-1-60374-961-9
Printed in the United States of America
© 2014 by Vanessa Miller

Whitaker House
1030 Hunt Valley Circle
New Kensington, PA 15068
www.whitakerhouse.com

Library of Congress Cataloging-in-Publication Data (Pending)

1 2 3 4 5 6 7 8 9 10 11 ᰃ 21 20 19 18 17 16 15 14

The Preacher

One

Twenty-five candles. The Morrison family wasn't just celebrating a birthday—they were celebrating life. Isaiah's sister Elaine was in remission. She leaned down and blew out the candles on her cake—a marbled mix of vanilla, coffee, and chocolate, just the way she liked it. She looked around the table and beamed with overflowing joy. "Thank you all for sharing this day with me."

Next to Elaine sat her husband, John—her hero. On her other side sat Natua, the adopted daughter of Isaiah's other sister, Dee Dee. Next to Natua was Drake, Dee Dee's husband. Their father, Joel, presided over the feast from the head of the table. And next to Isaiah sat Eric, the politician.

"I wonder why Shawn didn't come," Elaine said as she began cutting the cake and transferring the slices to dessert plates.

Dee Dee nervously glanced at Isaiah. He knew that she alone was aware of his struggle to adopt a forgiving attitude toward his younger brother since learning that Shawn—the playboy—had had an affair with Tanya, Isaiah's ex-wife. Granted, it had happened the summer before Isaiah had married her, but that didn't mitigate the sting.

Dee Dee then turned to John and quickly tried to move the conversation away from Shawn's absence. "That's a mighty big rock you put on Elaine's finger. If it weren't for your excellent taste in diamonds, I might still be annoyed with you for taking my sister off to Mexico and marrying her without any family there to witness it."

"Believe me, I would have preferred to marry Elaine in front of a thousand witnesses," John insisted. "But it took her so long to agree to marry me that I didn't want to wait another minute."

Elaine patted her husband's hand. "It's my fault, Dee Dee. I was so happy to be in remission, all I could think about was marrying the man I love. But I promise you, we will renew our vows in twenty years…and you, my dear sister, will be my bridesmaid."

"Okay, just as long as I get to pick out my own dress. I wouldn't be caught dead in the awful dresses some of my friends have been forced to wear."

Everyone laughed, Isaiah included. They all knew that Dee Dee meant what she said.

Isaiah nudged Eric. "Why didn't Linda come with you tonight?"

Eric averted his eyes. "She's not feeling well."

Dee Dee turned to Eric as if she had been invited into the conversation. "You really need to get her some help before she ruins your run for governor of Ohio."

"And you really need to mind your own business," Eric said with venom in his voice.

Isaiah held up his hands. "I wasn't trying to get an argument started. Can we please switch topics?"

Then Shawn walked into the dining room, and Isaiah—the preacher, the peacemaker—found that he was ready to rumble.

⌒

An eviction notice was taped to Ramona Verse's door when she got home after a series of disappointing events that would have broken the resolve of a weaker woman. But even after depositing her unemployment check and discovering that her bank balance was still in the negative, to the tune of $131—and even after lowering her standards by stepping into a cash-advance establishment and borrowing $500 to cover bank fees and pay her electric bill—she was still short and couldn't come close to paying her rent.

Dwayne Verse was the cause of all her problems. He'd promised to love, honor, and cherish her—before God, his mama, and a room full of folks who'd eaten up all the shrimp, beef, penne, and wedding cake they could get their hands on. All of them could be considered witnesses to the crime committed against her foolish heart.

Why hadn't any of those people told her that Dwayne needed a leash and a pooper-scooper? After all, they were feasting on food that her mother had needed to take out a loan in order to pay for. One of Dwayne's relatives could easily have pulled her to the side and said, "Hey, I don't mean to ruin your big day and all, but Dwayne is a thief and a cheater. You might want to make like the runaway bride and put some distance between you and this brother."

But even if someone had warned her, she probably wouldn't have listened. She had been young, dumb, and looking for love when she'd met Dwayne. He had been a member of her church choir, and his voice was so anointed that she'd naturally thought the rest of him would be, too. But that hadn't been the case. Ramona had quickly realized that she'd married a man with multiple personalities. The one he allowed almost everyone else to see was that of the "do-good" church boy. But the personality she'd become acquainted with was the one who lived high on the hog—at her expense. As a music teacher, Dwayne hadn't made much money, and Ramona's career as a financial planner had given him the income he'd always longed for.

He'd spent money like it was in endless supply. There had been no debt ceiling in the Verse household, not as long as Ramona had kept bringing home her paychecks and bonuses. But one day she'd come home from the office early and found Dwayne in bed with one of his fellow choir members. Then she'd found out about an affair he was having with a teacher at his school. Ramona was done.

However, she had somehow forgotten the lesson her grandmother had drilled into her head since she'd gone on her first date: "Don't never let a man know that you're leaving until you done left."

Everybody thought Grandma Bee had lost a piece of her mind when she'd had that stroke about twenty years ago, but that woman knew exactly what she was talking about. As Ramona sat at her kitchen table, eating a bologna sandwich on stale bread for dinner, she wished she had listened to Grandma Bee.

She'd boldly told Dwayne that she was filing for divorce and had given him a week to pack his stuff and get out of her house. But he hadn't needed a full week. Within two days, he'd packed up and left. He'd also taken the twenty grand that Ramona had managed to save over her years of hard work.

The next month, Ramona had been laid off. Since the economy was doing so poorly and people were barely scraping by, there was little demand for her services in financial planning. She'd had to put her house up for sale in a buyers' market and ended up doing a short sale just to get rid of the property.

In her years of working, Ramona would regularly advise her clients not to take money out of their 401(k)s, but she had been on unemployment and working temp assignments for six months now, and things weren't looking good. She'd made up her mind to contact the human resource department at her former company and take out a loan from her 401(k) account.

Yet before she was able to do that, she'd received a call from Christ Tabernacle about the résumé she'd submitted on one of the online employment sites. Pastor Isaiah Morrison was looking for a financial specialist to run a charity fund he was setting up in his father's honor. Ramona had gone on the interview and done everything but cross her fingers and hold her breath while trying to convince the pastor that she was the right person for the job. She'd prayed that he wouldn't perform a credit check or ask about her current finances, because they were a shambles. She needed the job and was prepared to beg.

Fortunately, Pastor Isaiah hadn't made her beg. After their brief discussion, he'd offered her the job on the spot. Ramona had wanted to jump up and hug the man. And she would have, if it hadn't been for the fact that Pastor Isaiah was the handsomest man she'd seen in her entire life. Ramona was positive that women came on to him all the time, pastor or not. She wasn't going to do anything that might cause her to lose the only job offer she'd gotten in months.

Two

Isaiah felt like a coward for hiding behind his office door, afraid to step out to even get a cup of coffee—and he really needed that coffee. If his brothers could see him now, Eric would laugh in his face, and Shawn would say that he was lame. But Isaiah no longer cared what Shawn said or thought. His sibling had betrayed him in the worst way possible, and although Isaiah preached forgiveness, he found it difficult to find any in his heart for his brother.

It if weren't for Shawn, Isaiah would be in the staff kitchen, getting himself a cup of coffee right now. But Shawn had opened his eyes to the fact that beautiful women could be treacherous. His ex-wife, Tanya, had taken him to school on that. Since learning that she had engaged in an affair with Shawn the summer before her wedding to Isaiah, and then discovering that his beautiful daughter, Erin, did not belong to him or even his brother but to one of Shawn's football teammates from college, Isaiah had been reeling. When Tanya had asked for a divorce so that she could be with Erin's *real* daddy, like a fool, he'd pleaded with her to stay.

In the end, Tanya had walked out anyway, taking his precious daughter and his crumpled pride. Isaiah felt like he'd been whupped by a heavyweight. He was tired of fighting and just wanted a little peace. But now he feared that the woman he'd just hired was about to disrupt his life in ways Tanya couldn't have even dreamed of doing.

He leaned back in his black leather chair and let his mind's eye travel back to the day Ramona had walked into his office, her big brown eyes imploring him to give her the job. And he had— without checking one single reference. He'd never thought of himself as the most gullible man who ever lived, but in truth, he had noticed more than her brown eyes that day. And everything he'd seen made him want to run in the opposite direction. Ramona wasn't cover-girl beautiful like Tanya. No, she had that girl-next-door type of beauty that made a man relax and let down his guard in her presence.

There was a knock outside his office. "Come in," Isaiah said.

The door opened, and his assistant, Tina Blackwood, stepped inside. "Just wanted to let you know that Ramona is getting settled in."

"Thank you for taking care of that for me, Tina. I've been here only three months, and I still feel a bit overwhelmed with all there is to know about the numerous projects and programs we have."

"But you served in leadership here for five years before taking over as pastor. Surely you knew about our programs."

"Knowing about them and being responsible for them are two different things. I'm reviewing each program to make sure that we have the right people leading it and to see what else we might be able to do to ensure its success." Isaiah rubbed his temples, and the stress drained from his face. "It doesn't help matters that my father tasked me with setting up this charity fund. I doubt if I'll have much time for Ms. Verse."

A knowing grin spread across Tina's round face. "Is this your sly way of asking me to work with Ramona? So you can get caught up with the 'work of the Lord'?" She'd elevated her voice dramatically, hands raised in the air.

Isaiah liked that Tina wasn't so sanctified that she couldn't crack a smile or a joke. This last year of his life had been pretty bleak, so he needed the joy that laughter could bring every now and then. "All kidding aside, Tina, I would appreciate it if you would manage this project and then report to me with proposals and potential organizations that she recommends we contribute to. Okay?"

Tina gave him a look that indicated what he was asking was way out of line. But instead of rejecting the idea outright, she planted her hands on her ample hips and said, "I don't mind working with her, as long as you understand that my work for this church has to come first."

"Of course. I would never ask you to neglect your duties for a personal project of mine." Isaiah sighed. "I just really need your help, Tina. So, if you can make time for Ms. Verse, I'd really appreciate it."

"Okay, Pastor. I know that you have a lot on your plate already, so don't worry. I'll help Ramona in whatever way she needs."

"Thank you."

"Not a problem." She turned and headed for the door.

"Hey, Tina?"

She spun around.

"Would you mind bringing me back a cup of coffee?"

She glared at him, then opened the door and said, in a saccharine voice, "Cream with two sugars, right?"

"Three sugars, please."

The door slammed behind her.

"I am lame," Isaiah admitted to himself, and laid his head on his desk.

Three

Pastor Isaiah was avoiding her. Ramona knew what that felt like, because her ex-husband had an avoidance personality. When Dwayne had lost his job, he'd stayed at his mother's house for three days just so he wouldn't have to admit to Ramona what had happened.

Whenever she'd tried to discuss their marital issues with him, Dwayne would act as if there was just too much work to do around the house for him to spend time chitchatting. Even with all of his avoidance issues, Ramona would gladly have stayed married to the man—if she hadn't discovered that he was also a thief and a cheat.

Pastor Isaiah was another matter altogether. He didn't seem like the type to skirt issues and practice denial. Ramona pictured him as the kind of guy who would be the last one standing at a press conference. He'd answer so many questions that the media would get tired and start accusing him of being too forthcoming. But what did she know? After all, she had married Dwayne Verse.

Ramona figured it was best that she keep her head down and do her job so she could continue collecting a salary. She'd been at the church for two weeks now. Her first paycheck wasn't due until next week, so she had moved out of her apartment, rather than live as a squatter until the sheriff threw her out on the street. She was now rooming with her cousin Mallory and making plans to pay off her past-due bills as quickly as possible so that she could get her own place again. The bonus she would receive, once she had managed to find suitable charitable organizations for Pastor Isaiah to contribute his considerable inheritance to, would certainly help.

Ramona had a meeting scheduled with Tina at 10:00 a.m. to discuss the list of agencies she would be recommending as prospective recipients of some of the foundation's money. She had spent her first weeks of employment diligently researching five agencies. Three of them had turned out to be bogus, but the other two seemed promising.

Since her employer wasn't giving her the time of day, and she had to communicate everything through Tina, Ramona had made doubly sure that the proposals she had put together included indisputable facts and figures. She didn't want to be accused of making decisions based on emotions rather than objective reason. However, Ramona was willing to admit the difficulty in not becoming emotional over some of the cases, such as the scores of children (and adults) in Somalia dying of hunger because of a famine. But it wasn't just the famine that was killing them. Rebel forces in the nation were intentionally preventing aid organizations from delivering food and water to help the citizens, because of their own sadistic need for money and power. Many of those rebel forces were on their way out of Somalia, but almost half of the population of 10 million had been affected, and Ramona believed their plight was a worthy cause, for reasons emotional and practical.

She was also hopeful that some of the money would be donated to an organization that provided funds to struggling single women. Ramona knew firsthand what a blessing a little help in times of need could be for a person. If someone had been there to pay her rent or her utilities while she tried to figure her way out of the bind her ex-husband had put her in, Ramona would have been eternally grateful.

A smile crept across her face as she grabbed the files off of her desk and headed for Tina's office. She had done her homework, and she was positive that Tina would be able to give a good report to her elusive boss. Whether at a church or in a corporate environment, Ramona knew all too well that not having access to the person who signed off on her reports and recommendations was detrimental to her success. So, she had determined to handle the funds in Pastor Isaiah's charity foundation with such skill that he would have no choice but to sit up and take notice.

She knocked on Tina's door and waited. When no summons came, Ramona glanced at her watch to make sure that she wasn't too early. No, she was right on time. She knocked again. Beverly, the church bookkeeper, poked her head out of the file room. "She's not here."

Ramona looked at her watch again, as if that would cause Tina to magically appear. "But...we have a meeting."

Beverly shrugged her shoulders. "Sorry. Her grandmother is gravely ill, so she left for Macon, Georgia, last night. I'm not sure when she'll be back."

"I'm sorry to hear that." Ramona turned and walked away from Tina's door. Back in her closet-sized office, she set her files on her desk and sat down. "Now what am I supposed to do?" she wondered out loud.

The organization that helped single women was holding a fund-raising dinner tomorrow night. She had secured two tickets to the dinner and had been hoping that Tina would give them to Pastor Isaiah. She had a feeling that if the pastor met the people heading the organization and heard for himself about the needs of these single women, he would be willing to contribute some of his considerable wealth to the cause.

Now what? Did she have to wait until Tina came back to give a report on the work she'd done so far? It didn't sound as if Tina would be back in time to ask Pastor Isaiah if he'd like to attend the fund-raising dinner that Ramona considered crucial in enlisting his help for the sake of thousands of women across the country.

The causes of the other organizations she was planning to recommend supporting were just as important—and just as urgent—as the single women's initiative. Ramona made a decision. She couldn't just sit there and wait on Tina to return.

She grabbed her files and headed for Pastor Isaiah's office. His door was ajar; through the opening, she could see him sitting behind his desk, his Bible open beside him, jotting down notes. Ramona was struck once again by how handsome this man was. She felt sorry for the women in his congregation—they must have a hard time concentrating on the message every Sunday, with fantasies and wedding plans for Pastor Isaiah simultaneously running through their heads.

Ramona had once known a woman who was convinced that God had told her she was supposed to marry Pastor Jones, the preacher at Ramona's former church. She'd reminded the woman that Pastor Jones was already married, but that hadn't daunted the woman or dampened her fantasy. She'd simply smiled and said, "That's why I've been taking cooking lessons. God showed me that Sister Jones is about to pass away, and while I'm consoling Pastor Jones and bringing him home-cooked meals, he'll discover that I am to be his new wife."

"Well," Ramona had replied, "I just hope that if your dream of marrying the pastor comes true, no one puts a spiritual hit out on you just so she can be wife number three."

Some people are just nuts, Ramona mused as she knocked on the doorjamb, trying her best to ignore the Denzel Washington lips and Morris Chestnut eyebrows on her boss as he glanced up. She gave the door a little push. "Do you have a moment, Pastor Isaiah?"

⌒

No! Isaiah wanted to scream. He didn't want to give this woman a moment, a second, or anything else. Every day of work over the last two weeks had been torture for him. Ramona's sweet, flowery fragrance always lingered in the corridor and followed him into his office, making it nearly impossible for him to concentrate on his job.

Isaiah now believed that he'd made a mistake by hiring this woman. It wasn't for lack of skills—her résumé had vouched for her considerable experience as a financial planner, and he had no doubt she would select viable organizations in which to invest his money. But he'd severely underestimated the effect she would have on him. He had tried to insulate himself by having her work with Tina, but now that Tina had gone to be with her grandmother, his first line of defense was defunct. He was a goner.

Ramona was standing at his door, looking like a vision in a light pink swing dress that clung to her waist and then flared out, managing to tastefully enhance every bump and curve she possessed. Yep, hiring her had been a bad idea.

He put down his pen and put on his best "I'm a busy man; don't bother me" facial expression. "What can I do for you, Ramona?"

She stepped into his office and stood in front of his desk, holding several files. He noticed that her hands were shaking slightly, and she appeared hesitant...scared. Had he said or done something to give her reason to fear him? He couldn't think of anything, especially since they'd barely interacted. He'd mostly tried to stay out of her way, so he couldn't imagine why she would be nervous in his presence. But that helpless look on her face cut him deep. He pointed at the chair next to his desk. "Have a seat, Ramona. I know Tina isn't here, but don't worry. I'll make time for whatever you need."

She audibly exhaled as she set the files on his desk. "Thank you, Pastor Isaiah. Some of the information I've researched is time sensitive, and I was hoping that I could have about thirty minutes of your attention."

Isaiah glanced at his watch and then nodded. "That should be okay. What's up?"

Getting down to business, she sat down and opened one of the folders she'd placed on his desk. "First, we need to discuss the investment strategy that I think will work best for your foundation."

"Investment strategy?" Isaiah almost laughed. "The Dow plunged six hundred thirty-five points the other day."

"Yeah, but it soared four hundred thirty points the very next day. Plus, the Federal Reserve has vowed to keep interest rates low, and that's always good for stocks." She pointed to a graph on the first page of her proposal. "But, even with that said, I am recommending that you put about fifty-eight percent of the money in U.S. Treasury bonds. Then we'll play the stock market with the other forty-two percent."

Isaiah leaned back in his chair, distancing himself from Ramona's distracting presence. He needed to decide what to do with the money his father had entrusted him to give away. And although a hundred million was a considerable sum of money, if he really wanted to do some good, he'd need to grow that money first—hence the investment portfolio he'd asked Ramona to put together. But now he wondered if he could trust her recommendation. "With all the upheaval in the government right now, do you really think we should put so much money in Treasury bonds?"

She lifted her hands as if to stop his train of thought. "I know where you're going, but even with the economic uncertainty, Treasury bonds are still a safe bet."

"I don't know," Isaiah said. "Those people seem crazy enough to bring down the government, if you ask me."

"Okay, if the Tea Party makes you nervous, we can put about thirty-eight percent in Treasury bonds, twenty percent in gold, and the other forty-two percent in stocks. And then, once the Tea

Party is voted out of Congress, we'll move a little more money into bonds."

"How much do you recommend we invest?"

"Well, since you want to begin giving money away immediately, there's no way that you can invest it all. And, considering your current mood about stocks and bonds, I think you'd be very uncomfortable investing even half of it at this point."

Isaiah began to relax a bit. He liked the fact that Ramona was listening to his concerns and then adapting her proposal to fit him, rather than sticking with her preconceived notions of how the investing should be done.

"So, my recommendation," Ramona continued, "is that we start out by investing twenty percent of the portfolio. That way, you'll have more money free and ready for the job at hand."

"I like your thought process so far. Have you found any organizations that seem worthy of funding?" Isaiah was enjoying this conversation. He wondered why in the world he had been so afraid to sit down and talk to Ramona in the first place.

She closed the investment folder and opened one of the others she'd brought with her. "So far I've researched five and found two to be promising. I have provided you with a proposal for each of my recommendations."

Isaiah thumbed through the paperwork as Ramona continued.

"The first proposal concerns the famine in Somalia. Almost three hundred thousand children under the age of five have already died. I thought you might like to contribute to an organization that is providing relief in the form of food and water."

"You were right about that. But I thought the Somali pirates or Al-Qaeda members weren't allowing anyone in."

Ramona nodded. "The rebels have left the capital, making it easier to get supplies into the country. But we would need to hurry, because the rebels could return at any time."

Isaiah couldn't believe how quickly she'd convinced him. "Okay, I think you're right—we should support this organization. I trust that you've vetted it thoroughly. Send ten thousand for now, and if they are able to get the food and water to the people without any mishaps, then we'll give more." He put down the papers he'd been going through. "Tell me about the other organization."

Her eyes lit up. "Women Moving Up, or WMU, is working to stamp out poverty among single women, especially single mothers."

"You seem pretty excited about this organization." Isaiah liked the way Ramona smiled. It made him feel all warm inside.

"I am. I may not be a parent, but I know something about being single and not having enough money to meet my needs." She reached inside her pocket and pulled out two small pieces of paper. "They're having a fund-raising dinner tomorrow night, and I was able to reserve two tickets, in case you wanted to check them out further." She laid them on his desk. "It's black tie...probably a nice event."

He picked up the tickets. "You really think I should attend this thing?"

"I think you owe it to yourself to find out more about this organization. Maybe you'll come to feel as strongly about support-ing it as I do." She stood. "Look, I don't want to take up any more of your time. I have some more organizations I need to research, so I'll just leave you with the information I've gathered so far."

Isaiah looked at the tickets again as Ramona walked toward the door. Tomorrow was Friday. As usual, he had no plans for the evening. Hadn't had any plans since Tanya left him, over a year ago. And now he had not just one but two tickets for a formal affair. He needed a date.

He glanced up just as Ramona put her hand on the doorknob. "What am I supposed to do with the other ticket?"

She turned around to face him. "Whatever you want. You can go alone, or you can invite someone."

Isaiah stood up and walked around his desk, closing the distance between them. He wasn't sure what was driving him to do this, but he just couldn't help himself. In a husky voice he hardly recognized, he said, "Are you busy tomorrow night?"

Her eyes widened. "Me?"

"Yeah, you. After all, you're the one who got me into this thing. I'm not comfortable at formal events, so I sure don't want to go alone."

She lowered her eyes and rubbed her temple. He sure hoped she wouldn't turn him down.

"What's it going to be, Ramona? If you're not going, then neither am I."

She met his gaze. "I don't have a dress," she admitted.

His heart sank. He tried to hand her back the tickets. "Then just tell them we can't make it."

Her eyes widened. "Oh, no. You have to attend. Don't worry— I'll find something to wear."

Four

I t is more blessed to give than to receive"—that's what the Bible said, and Ramona was so thankful that some woman had decided to give this stylish two-tone dress with a French designer label to the local Goodwill. She twirled around in front of the full-length mirror in the corner of the bedroom. For dinner out with her boss, this dress was prefect. It was sleeveless, but it had a high collar, so no one could accuse her of trying to tempt the pastor by showing off her cleavage. The design of the bodice paired well with the silky skirt's high waistline. Sleek sashes draped down the neckline and ran across the bodice. It was a dress that spoke of business and pleasure at the same time. The icing on the cake for Ramona was the fact that she'd paid only four bucks for it!

She pinned her hair on top of her head, allowing a few errant curls to fall out. Then she applied her makeup—eye shadow, foundation, lipstick, and mascara. Finished, Ramona grabbed her evening bag and sat down in the living room to wait for her date to arrive. She reminded herself that Pastor Isaiah wasn't actually her "date"; this was a business outing. And she planned to focus her energies this evening on convincing Pastor Isaiah of what a worthy cause the women's group was.

The doorbell rang, and she jumped up like a giddy school-girl. *What on earth is the matter with you?* she chided herself. *Calm down.* Taking a deep breath to slow her pulse, she opened the front door and watched Mr. Beautiful saunter into her world.

⟲

Isaiah knew he was in trouble the moment he walked into the house and saw Ramona. He couldn't take his eyes off of her. The dress she was wearing was simple yet stunning, especially the way it clung to every curve she possessed. *Stop that.* He blinked and then managed to turn his attention to photos on the coffee table. "Family?"

Ramona nodded. "That's my aunt and uncle. This is my cousin's house. I'm staying with her until I can get a few bills straightened out, and then I'll buy a place of my own."

That was a surprise. "Somehow I imagined that a financial planner would have her finances in order at all times."

"That is the goal," Ramona assured him. "But sometimes the unavoidable happens and moves the goalpost."

Isaiah was impressed by this woman. She didn't try to pretend that she was something she wasn't. After dealing with Tanya's deceit, he needed a woman who could be real with him. He glanced at her dress again as he remembered that she'd told him she didn't have any formal wear. "That dress must have set the goalpost back a bit."

Ramona laughed. "Don't worry; my budget can handle the expense of a pre-owned dress."

Again, Isaiah was struck by this woman's honesty. Tanya never would have admitted to anyone that she'd purchased a dress secondhand. Maybe—just maybe—God was trying to show him something about the exquisite woman in front of him. "Let's get going," he said. "I'm anxious to find out a bit more about this organization."

They arrived at the banquet center just as the butler-served hors d'oeuvre hour was ending and the other guests were taking their seats around the circular tables in the ballroom. Isaiah found two available spots, and he and Ramona sat down, just as salad plates were placed in front of them. During the meal, they enjoyed pleasant conversation with the other guests at their table.

As the servers began clearing the dinner plates and distributing dessert, the president of WMU took her place behind the podium. Isaiah listened intently to everything she had to say. She was an impressive woman. With three small children and no husband, she had worked her way from welfare to college to corporate America, and then to entrepreneurship. She had faith in the women of America and believed that with God's help, other single mothers could accomplish what she had—and more.

Isaiah leaned over and whispered in Ramona's ear, "I like her style. Do you think she'll speak with us at the end of the event?"

"I'm sure she will," Ramona whispered back. "I'll try to set something up once she sits down."

"Hey, Big Bro! I thought that was you."

The voice was like fingernails on a chalkboard. Isaiah didn't have to lift his head to know that Shawn stood next to him, grinning like the Grinch who stole Christmas. His good mood vanished, and he jumped out of his seat, bumping against the table and overturning his iced tea, which spilled all over Ramona.

She leaped up, mouth open wide.

"Ramona, I'm so sorry." Isaiah grabbed his napkin and attempted to wipe her front. When he realized he was touching areas that he shouldn't, he handed her the napkin and stepped back. "I'm sorry," he said again.

The little episode had drawn the attention of everyone, including the WMU president, who stopped speaking. Head down in embarrassment, Ramona grabbed her purse. "I'm going to the bathroom to see if I can clean this up," she told Isaiah, then turned and hustled out of the ballroom.

As the president resumed her speech, Isaiah went after Ramona, with Shawn on his heels.

"What are you doing here?" Isaiah demanded once they were standing outside the women's restroom, out of earshot and eyesight of everyone else.

"Same thing you're doing here, I guess…trying to find some place to unload Daddy's loot."

He was so glib, so nonchalant, about everything, and it made Isaiah sick.

"Who's the woman? Are you dating again?"

Did Shawn really think that he was about to discuss his personal life with the man who'd slept with his fiancée? The boy must have been hit in the head too many times on that football field. "Why'd you have to come over to my table and bother me?"

"You are my brother, in case you've forgotten."

"I wish I could forget," Isaiah snapped. "Just stay away from me."

"Look, I didn't want to fight with you. I actually do have something to tell you. It's about Tanya and Erin."

"You keep Tanya and Erin out of your mouth." Isaiah turned and started to walk away.

Shawn stopped him with a hand on his shoulder. "Cal is not Erin's father. The DNA test came back last week."

Isaiah wrenched out of his grasp as the door to the ladies' restroom opened. He stood there for a moment, too stunned to move. Tanya's deception had cost his daughter another father. "So, I guess you're happy that you and your friend are in the clear?"

Shawn lifted his hands. "Hey, man, Erin's not mine. Don't expect me to be sad about not having a baby by my brother's ex-wife."

"Yeah, but she could have been yours."

"Evidently, there are a lot of children in that category," Shawn groused.

Ramona cleared her throat loudly. "Are you ready to go back to our seats?"

"No." Isaiah grabbed her arm and led her away from his brother. "Let's get out of here."

"But I thought you wanted to speak with the president of WMU."

He looked over his shoulder and glared daggers at Shawn. "Not anymore—not if my brother's a donor. He has a habit of turning women into single mothers, so I guess it's only fair."

Five

I'm sorry about what happened back there," Isaiah said to Ramona as he drove out of the parking lot. "My brother and I just don't mix well anymore."

Ramona didn't know if she should pretend that she hadn't heard as much of the conversation as she had—not that anyone could have missed what was said—or if she should come right out and admit that every bit of what she'd heard had broken her heart for the humble, God-fearing man who was Isaiah Morrison.

"I'm embarrassed to have lost control like that," Isaiah continued.

"I'd say you had a good reason to be upset."

They rode in silence until he pulled up in front of Ramona's cousin's house and let out a long sigh. "So, you know about what happened to my family?"

She hesitated. "I'd heard bits and pieces of why you and your ex-wife divorced, but I had no idea that your brother had anything to do with it."

Isaiah nodded. "I want to forgive him, I really do. But every time I see him, I'm reminded of his betrayal, and the pain only gets worse. Especially when I'm the guy who always had his back, no matter what crazy thing he'd gotten himself into."

Ramona gave a sympathetic shake of her head. "What happened to you is pretty bad, but I believe that forgiveness is a choice," she said, trying to bring some hope into the conversation. "You have to make a conscious choice to forgive the person who wronged you, and then you'll begin to see a change in the way you feel." She added shyly, "That's what I believe, anyway."

He eyed her. "That's easy for you to say. You've never been married."

Ramona opened her mouth to tell Isaiah that she had, in fact, been married and endured a painful divorce, just as he had. But then she remembered that the day she'd filled out her application for the position at Isaiah's church, she'd been so furious with her ex-husband that she'd wanted to wipe the memory of his existence from her life. So, on her job application and related paperwork, she'd identified herself as "Miss" Ramona Verse rather than "Mrs." or "Ms."

Even though she wanted to tell him the truth, she couldn't afford to admit that she'd lied on her application and risk losing her job—not when she was finally getting her life back in order after that loser of an ex-husband tried to rip everything apart. She decided to keep the secret to herself, and prayed that one day she would find the courage to tell Isaiah why she'd been dishonest about her marital status. "You may have the best job in the world, being that you've got a hotline to heaven, but I read my Bible and pray, too. And whether you believe it or not, I do know a little something about forgiveness," she said.

The corners of Isaiah's lips curved upward in a smile. "I don't know if I have the best job in the world," he said. "Sometimes being a preacher is stifling."

"I'm surprised to hear you say that. The way you preach, I can't imagine you doing anything else."

He shrugged. "Don't get me wrong, I love what I do; I wouldn't choose any other career, nor do I think the Lord would want me to. It's just that…well, I'm not as free to do certain things."

"Like what?"

He turned and looked at her. It was in that moment that she saw the heat in his gaze. A fire was raging in those dark eyes of his, and it was raging for her.

"Well, before I became a pastor, when I couldn't get a woman off my mind, I would tell her. And when the lingering scent of her perfume was so intoxicating that the fragrance stayed with me for hours after I left her presence, I would let her know that, too."

Stunned by Isaiah's admission, all she could say was, "Oh."

He held up his hands, as if backing off. "I'm not trying to make a move on you, Ramona. It's just…well, I would like to get to know you better. But this stuff is all new to me. I haven't dated since the last millennium, and now I'm a divorced preacher. I don't know the rules."

Ramona straightened her shoulders. "Well, I think that if a single man is interested in a single woman, then he should ask her out…whether he's a preacher, a businessman, or whatever."

He leaned back against the headrest and studied her. "You speak your mind. I like that about you."

"Life is too short to play games. I believe that people should say what they mean and mean what they say."

He looked down at her dress and nodded. "You didn't get the spot out."

She shrugged. "I got most of it out. For four dollars, I don't care if I never wear this dress again."

"But it looks so nice on you. I'm sorry again that I messed it up. I'll make it up to you somehow."

She giggled. "There's nothing to make up."

"We'll see." He leaned over and kissed her cheek. The effect was electrifying. "What are you doing tomorrow?"

She had to catch her breath before she could speak. Never in her life had a simple kiss on the cheek been so powerful. And now he was asking what she had going on tomorrow. Was he asking her out? Should she accept? It would be nice to have someone to share the day with. She'd spent so many days alone, and tomorrow was her birthday—the one day she'd rather not spend in solitude. "N-nothing much…just hanging around the house," she replied, feigning nonchalance.

He got out of the car and walked around to her side, opened the passenger door, and held out his hand. Ramona took it and stepped out. "Thanks for coming with me," Isaiah said as he closed the door.

"Thanks for inviting me. I had a good time."

He gave her a scolding frown. "No need to lie, Miss Verse."

"No, I'm serious. I really did enjoy the event."

"Until I spilled my iced tea on you and then rushed you to the car as if the building was about to blow up."

She chuckled. "There was that."

Isaiah put his hands in his pockets and walked her to the front door. He waited for her to pull the key out of her purse and put it in the lock. When Ramona looked back at him, she saw something else in his eyes, as if he wanted to say more. But when nothing came out of his mouth, she waved and said, "Well, see ya."

As if awakened from a trance, he took his hands out of his pockets and waved back. "Yeah, okay."

The next morning, Ramona was sitting at the dining room table in her peach-colored pajamas, munching on Apple Jacks cereal and sipping orange juice, when her cousin Mallory came downstairs. She poured herself a bowl of Apple Jacks and then sat down at the table across from her. "So, do you have anything fun planned for today?"

"Same old fun I have every Saturday…paying bills and reviewing my debt-to-income ratio."

Mallory frowned. "Come on, Ramona. You do that depressing stuff every Saturday. Don't you think you should do something special for yourself today?"

"I don't have money to do anything special. I don't even have enough money to do something ordinary."

Mallory finished her cereal, took the bowl to the sink, and poured out the extra milk. She leaned against the sink and turned to face Ramona. "I don't know how you do it."

"Do what?"

"Dwayne stole everything from you, and then you lost your job and your house, and you're digging yourself out of a mound of debt, but you don't seem bitter...I just don't get it."

Ramona took her bowl to the sink and rinsed it out. "Life's too short for bitterness, Mal. Sure, some bad things have happened to me, and some days I am truly ticked off about it. But when I read my Bible or listen to messages on God's goodness, I'm reminded that I'm not in this alone. God's got this...I'm just along for the ride."

"If you say so." Mallory reached inside the oversized pocket of her housecoat and pulled out an envelope. "Happy birthday, Cuz," she said, handing it to Ramona.

Smiling, Ramona took the card and hugged her cousin. "Thanks, girl. At least somebody remembered that I was born today."

"Well, I've got a bunch of errands to run. I'll see you later, okay? If you're not doing anything tonight, I'd love to take you to dinner to celebrate."

After Mallory had left, Ramona sat down in the living room with a handful of envelopes, a calculator, her checkbook, and a notepad. She would receive a paycheck next week, so she would be able to pay one of her past-due bills. Mallory hadn't charged her rent last month because she'd moved in after the rent had already been paid. But soon she would need to write a check for her portion of the rent and utilities. Adding rent to the mix would leave her with less money to put toward the bills she and Dwayne owed, but she needed a place to lay her head, and nobody but her mama would allow her to stay for free. But her mama lived three hundred miles away. Ramona was grateful that Mallory was willing to share her home with her, and she wouldn't dream of taking advantage of her cousin's kindness.

She opened a few envelopes and pulled out the bills, laid them on the table, and picked up her notepad. Once a month, Ramona wrote down how much she owed on each of her past-due bills, then figured out how much money she had coming in that month and how much was going toward her current bills. Whatever was left went toward paying off a past-due bill. If she kept her system going, Ramona figured she'd be debt free within eighteen months.

Suddenly she noticed the doorbell ringing. She wasn't sure how long it had been doing that, since she'd been so consumed by her bill-paying process. Putting her pen down, she got up and went to the door. She looked through the peephole and saw a twenty-something blonde woman wearing a huge smile and holding a garment bag.

"Can I help you?" Ramona asked from behind the locked door. She was a firm believer in leaving salespeople and strangers on the porch and keeping the door locked—you never knew if they would try to get in the house so they could tie you up and steal everything in sight.

"I'm looking for Ramona Verse," the woman said.

"What can I do for you?" Ramona asked, still standing behind the locked door.

"Pastor Isaiah asked me to bring this stuff to you."

At the mention of Isaiah's name, Ramona's pulse accelerated, and she flung the door open. "Pastor Isaiah? What did he send me?"

The woman held out her hand to Ramona. "My name is Vicki Dole. I'm a personal shopper."

Ramona shook the woman's hand.

"Can I come in so I can show you the items that were pur-chased for you?"

Ramona opened the door wider, shaking her head in con-fusion. "I'm not sure I understand," she told the woman as she stepped into the living room.

Vicki handed her an envelope. "This might clear things up. You go ahead and read that while I open this garment bag, and then we can get down to business."

Ramona opened the envelope and pulled out a card with the words "Happy Birthday" scrawled in big bold letters across the front. She would say this for Pastor Isaiah—he sure knew how to read a job application. He'd called her "Miss Verse," and he must have seen her birth date in the section designed for purposes of a background check, even though he'd told her one wouldn't be necessary.

"Well, what do you think?"

Ramona turned and saw Vicki gesturing at the sofa. Her jaw dropped. There lay four evening gowns of various styles and colors, all of them equally stunning. She was speechless.

"They're all a size six," Vicki said. "I hope that was right. Pastor Isaiah's guess, of course"—she eyed Ramona up and down—"but I think they should work."

Ramona could only nod. "What—?" she attempted. "How—?"

Vicki shook her head. "Don't ask me. I'm just the delivery girl."

Remembering the card in her hand, Ramona opened it and read:

Ramona,

A beautiful woman like you should have dozens of gowns at her disposal. So, to replace the one I ruined, I've purchased four more. I would be ever so grateful if you wore one of them tonight, because I'd love to take you to dinner to celebrate your birthday.

Isaiah

Ramona nearly screamed for joy. He'd wanted to ask her out, after all. She'd thought that he was going to ask her when he dropped her off last night, but when he didn't say anything beyond asking about her plans, Ramona assumed that she'd been engaging in wishful thinking. But she had been right. He did want to go out with her. She had a date…on her birthday.

She wanted to dance around the room, but she had company. She turned back to Vicki. "Which one of these dresses should I wear for a dinner date?"

Six

It was her birthday, and she was going on a date. She had four dresses to choose from, and shoes and accessories to match. Two flowed all the way to the floor; the other two were knee length. Isaiah wasn't taking her to the opera or some other formal affair, so the floor-length dresses were out. Of the other two dresses he had sent, Ramona thought the lime green one would look sensational on her, with its halter top, pleated waist, and rhinestone buckle. Plus, its clingy style suited her figure. She felt like a princess as she slipped on the gorgeous gown.

Part of her wanted to pack everything up and send it back to Isaiah. She wasn't in a relationship with this man and didn't feel that it was right to accept such lavish gifts from him. But, as she noticed how the dress swayed on her as she stood in front of the full-length mirror, she reminded herself—again—that today was her birthday, and it had been years since she'd received a birthday present from anyone. Her ex-husband had never remembered the month of her birthday, let alone the day. So, why shouldn't she enjoy this one act of kindness bestowed on her?

Before she had time to ponder her dilemma any further, the doorbell rang. She glanced at her reflection one last time, tucked a strand of hair back in place, and then went to answer the door.

She opened it wide and stepped back so that Isaiah could walk in.

He took one look at her and said, "Beautiful."

Ramona assumed he was referring to the dress. She twirled around. "You like?"

He nodded and gulped. "I like it all," he almost whispered.

Ramona stumbled as she tried to right herself from the twirling she'd just done. And the look in Isaiah's eyes put her off balance again. She couldn't remember Dwayne ever looking at her like that...like she was water in a desert land.

"I can't believe I tried to avoid you...to act like you didn't matter," Isaiah murmured.

Now on firm footing, Ramona pointed at him and raised her eyebrows. "I knew you were avoiding me. But I thought you were thinking about firing me or something."

Isaiah laughed. "If I had fired you, I'd have to do all the work for my father's foundation myself. And although I believe what he's asked us to do is a worthy cause, I'd much rather spend my time on my ministry."

She was without words. This fine man was standing in her cousin's living room, admitting that he had feelings for her—on her birthday, no less. The dresses and accessories had been nice, but this right here...this was the real present.

Isaiah held up a hand. "I'm not trying to make a move on you."

Why not? she wanted to ask.

"I've been divorced for about a year now, and I'm still healing from all the drama my ex-wife took me through. But I want you to know that I'm tired of trying to avoid you. I want to be a part of your life. And if you can give me some time to work out the things I'm dealing with, I would then be able to tell you all that is in my heart. Can you give me some time, Ramona?"

Since the day she'd met Pastor Isaiah, Ramona had been drawn to him. There was just something about the bruised and battered man of God that she found attractive. It wasn't just his looks, either; although the man was fine. Ramona found herself attracted to his quiet strength, his humility, and the respect with which he treated others. In fact, until yesterday, she'd never heard him raise his voice at anyone. She didn't need to think long about whether or not she wanted to wait for Isaiah. She knew already. "Yeah, I think I can do that."

As if he had been holding his breath in anticipation of her answer, Isaiah exhaled. "Thank you," he said, then held out his hand. When she took his hand, he added, "And now, I'd like to take a pretty lady out to celebrate her birthday."

It hadn't been such a good idea to take Ramona out to dinner. Isaiah was now left with the memory of her smiling face...of the sound of her laughter...of the look in her eyes when he'd expressed his interest in her. The evening had been wonderful, but when it was over, he'd left her at her front door without so much as a good-night kiss.

Isaiah had wanted desperately to touch his lips to Ramona's soft, welcoming mouth. But he couldn't do that to her—not when he wasn't ready to commit to a relationship. Not when he had so many issues that needed to be resolved.

Ramona had knocked him off focus. He had worked all week on a message about God's ability to forgive and bring the sinful man back into right standing with Him. But by the time he'd climbed into the pulpit the Sunday after he'd taken her out, everything had gotten turned upside down. Before reading the Scripture passage he'd selected for the morning message, he'd stolen a quick glance at the balcony, where Ramona had been sitting since she'd started attending his church, and that was all it took. Instead of talking to his congregation about God bringing the sinful man back into the fold, he'd turned in his Bible to the fifth chapter of Matthew and read aloud, beginning with verse 27:

> *Ye have heard that it was said by them of old time, Thou shalt not commit adultery: but I say unto you, that whosoever*

*looketh on a woman to lust after her hath committed adultery
with her already in his heart. And if thy right eye offend thee,
pluck it out, and cast it from thee: for it is profitable for thee
that one of thy members should perish, and not that thy whole
body should be cast into hell. And if thy right hand offend thee,
cut it off, and cast it from thee: for it is profitable for thee that
one of thy members should perish, and not that thy whole body
should be cast into hell.*

Ever since delivering that sermon on "sin begins in the heart"
several days ago, he hadn't been able to look Ramona in the eye.
Right now, he was sitting in his office, contemplating plucking
out his eye and cutting off his arm. But then he realized that it
wasn't just the right eye or arm that offended him; he lusted after
Ramona with both eyes and wouldn't mind laying holy hands on
her, in a most unholy fashion. So, he had been keeping himself
locked away in his office again, never venturing out—not even for
coffee.

Someone knocked on his door. Isaiah put his pen down and
prayed that it wasn't Ramona—the one person he didn't want to
see. "Come in?" It sounded like a question, the way his voice rose
in pitch due to his panic.

As the door opened, he remembered that there was another
person he didn't want to see—Tanya. "What are you doing here?"
he asked as she closed the door behind her.

Dressed in a red business suit that clung to her like a second
skin, Tanya strutted into his office and perched in the empty chair
facing his desk. He hadn't seen this woman since the day after he
signed the divorce papers, when she came to his house to inform
him that she was moving with his daughter to Florida. He hadn't
known at the time that she had selected their destination because
she had convinced Cal Davis of the Tampa Bay Buccaneers that he
was Erin's father.

Cal had been successful in his football career, winning two Super Bowl rings and earning millions of dollars. He was currently divorcing his wife because they couldn't get along and she hadn't been able to have children. So, when he'd found out about Erin, he'd been thrilled. Too bad none of it was real.

"Hi, Isaiah. I hope this isn't a bad time."

As if you care. That's what he wanted to say, but good manners and home training had conditioned him to say, "I was working on something, but I can spare a few minutes."

She lowered her eyes and put her hands in her lap. She appeared to hesitate before saying, "I think I made a mistake."

Ya think? "What mistake are you referring to, Tanya?"

"The divorce. You didn't want it, and I think you were right. Erin is very unhappy without you in her life."

"I miss Erin too. Are you saying you're finally willing to let me see her?"

She looked at him with a warmth he hadn't seen in years. "Erin wants to come home, Isaiah…and so do I."

He didn't have time to play this game with her. He shook his head. "I already know that Cal threw you out. It appears that Erin isn't his biological daughter, either."

"How do you know that?"

"That's not your concern; just know that Erin is welcome to come home anytime she wants. But you no longer have a home with me." He narrowed his eyes. "Are we clear on that?"

"You don't have to be so mean, Isaiah. You did love me once. We shared a life together, remember?"

Without answering her, he stood up, walked to the door, and opened it. "It was nice seeing you, Tanya. Please bring Erin with you next time."

She swiveled around in the chair and gave him a look as if she had the upper hand and was about to let him know it. "Erin's out in the car."

"Why didn't you bring her in?"

"I needed to talk to you first, to remind you that you aren't off the hook for child support."

"You don't need to remind me of that. I signed her birth certificate. I've been there for her since the day she was born, and always will be. I don't have a problem paying child support."

She stood up and joined him at the door. "Erin's bags are already packed. She's expecting to spend a month with you while I find us another place to live."

"Just a minute ago, you were asking to live with me."

She shrugged. "I figured I'd give it a try."

He closed his eyes and counted to ten, in an attempt to rein in his temper. When he opened them again, he simply said, "Can you please go get her?"

"Not just yet. First I need something from you."

"Surprise, surprise."

"No need to be sarcastic, Isaiah. I'm just asking for what's rightfully mine. You owe me alimony and you know it."

"You declined the alimony, remember? As a matter of fact, you informed me that your man had more than enough money to take care of you."

Tanya waved a hand in the air dismissively. "That was then, and this is now."

"You mean, now that he's thrown you out."

"Whatever. Look, all I want to know is, do you want to spend time with Erin or not?"

"Of course I do."

"Then giving me the money shouldn't be a problem. After all, Erin will benefit, too."

"I'll pay alimony for one year. That's it. Now let me see my daughter."

"My goodness, Isaiah, calm down." She pointed to his desk. "You go back over there and write out my first check, and I'll go bring Erin in from the car."

As Tanya left his office, Isaiah sat down behind his desk and pulled out his checkbook like an obedient pup. What could he do but pay up? It was his fault that he'd married a deceptive woman like Tanya—a woman who would deliberately keep his child from him if he didn't agree to give her the sun, moon, and more, if she asked.

There was another knock on his open door. Isaiah looked up. Ramona was standing there, giving him a smile that spoke volumes.

"Hey," he said.

"Hey, yourself." She stepped inside. "Are you okay?"

"You heard that, huh?"

"Not all of it, but I was in the copy room when you opened the door." She lifted her shoulders with a sheepish smile. "It would have been kind of hard not to hear."

He leaned back in his chair, check in hand. "Well, at least I'll get to see my daughter."

"You're a good man, Isaiah Morrison." Ramona spoke the words with so much affection that it compelled him to stand up and walk to her.

"Who the heck are you?"

Isaiah and Ramona jumped away from each other like two kindergarteners caught kissing by the principal during recess. They turned to the door, where Tanya and Erin stood. Erin had a big grin on her face as she looked at her daddy. Tanya glared at Ramona like a woman scorned.

Seven

Ramona had the distinct impression that she needed to get out of Isaiah's office before this woman did her bodily harm. Then again, Ramona didn't like Isaiah's ex-wife very much. Based on the conversation she'd just overheard, the woman was an extortionist and a not-so-very-nice person. Putting her hand on her hip and letting her backbone slip, she said, "I'm Ramona Verse, and you are?"

Tanya flung her hand in the air. "Don't play games with me. Everybody in this church knows that I'm Isaiah's wife."

"Ex-wife," Isaiah corrected her.

"Whatever." Dismissing him with another wave of her hand, Tanya turned back to Ramona. "Don't nobody know better than me what a good man Isaiah is. And he don't need no church groupie telling him things I've already told him."

Ramona wouldn't deign to answer her. She turned to Isaiah. "I need to get back to work."

"Wait a minute, Ramona. Tanya was just leaving. All she's doing is dropping off my daughter." Isaiah shoved a check in his ex-wife's hand. "Isn't that right, Tanya?"

She rolled her eyes heavenward but didn't contradict him. Bending down, she gave Erin a hug and a kiss. "Now, you be good while you're with Daddy. I'll be back to get you as soon as I find us another place to live."

"Okay," Erin said, then rushed into Isaiah's waiting arms.

"I'll let you know if I need more," Tanya said, tucking the check in her purse. Then she turned and strutted out of the office.

Ramona wanted to snatch that check out of the woman's purse and tear it into a hundred little pieces, letting the confetti rain down on her money-grubbing head. But Isaiah didn't seem to care that he was being shaken like a piggy bank. She, who hardly knew the situation, was wearing a scowl of outrage, yet all she saw on Isaiah's face was love—love for the little girl he now held in his arms. Blood and DNA tests didn't mean anything to Isaiah. This was his daughter, and he would pay any price to have her with him.

Ramona couldn't fault him for loving his daughter. If her own father had loved her enough to stay in her life, maybe she would have made better choices when it came to the men she dated. Maybe she wouldn't be divorced and living on peanut butter and Ramen noodles.

Finally Isaiah set Erin down. "I missed you, Kiddo."

"I missed you too, Daddy." She grinned. "I'm glad Mommy has to find another place to live."

Ramona smiled. Children were such truth tellers. They said what they felt without worrying about how anyone else would perceive their words.

Isaiah turned Erin to face Ramona. "I'd like you to meet Miss Ramona Verse. She works here at the church."

Erin smiled shyly. "Hi, Miss Ramona."

Ramona grinned back. "Hi, Erin. It's really nice to meet you."

"Do you like working at the church with my daddy?"

Ramona glanced at Isaiah. He winked at her. "Yeah, I do like working with your daddy."

"When I grow up, I want to work with my daddy too."

"Oh, really? How old are you?"

"I'm eight," Erin said. "How old are you?"

Ramona's mouth opened, but nothing came out. She rarely heard that question, and, truthfully, once she'd passed twenty-five, she hadn't wanted to admit it to anyone.

"Whoa." Isaiah picked up his daughter again and swung her onto his back. "Come on, Kiddo. I'm taking you to lunch so you can stop asking pretty ladies embarrassing questions."

Ramona watched them trot out of the office. She followed them down the hall, heading back to her own office.

"What's the big deal?" she heard Erin say, still riding on Isaiah's back.

"Women don't like being asked their age," Isaiah tried to explain.

"She can't be that old," Erin said.

"I'm thirty-one," Ramona admitted.

Isaiah stopped so fast that Erin slid down his back, landing on her feet. He turned to face Ramona.

"Don't act so surprised," she said. "You've done your research."

He shook his head. "I know. I just didn't think you would admit it. I've never...I mean, most of the women I know refuse to tell anyone their age."

Ramona straightened her shoulders. "Then I guess I'm not like most of the women you know."

"Maybe you're not," Isaiah said, still staring at her as if he couldn't believe what he was seeing.

Erin tugged on his arm. "Daddy, Daddy, can Miss Ramona go to lunch with us?"

Ramona waved a hand in the air. "Oh no, I don't want to intrude on your father/daughter time."

Isaiah walked toward her, closing the gap between them. "You just heard my daughter. She wants you to come with us. And although I didn't read this on your application, I don't think you're the kind of woman who goes around disappointing kids."

"That was a low blow," she told him, then turned to Erin and smiled. "I would love to have lunch with you and your daddy. Thank you for asking. Just let me go to my office and get my purse."

"You won't need it," Isaiah told her. "My daddy would skin me alive if I allowed you to pay for your own meal."

She gave him a look that said, *"Mama didn't raise no fool."* "I wasn't planning on paying for my meal, but a girl does need to reapply lip gloss every now and then."

"Oh. Well, we'll wait for you to get your purse."

Ramona had to remind herself to walk, not run. When Isaiah hadn't asked her out again after her birthday, she had begun to think he had just been being nice to the lonely woman who worked for him, not wanting her—or anyone—to spend a birthday alone. But the way he'd looked at her just now gave her reason to hope.

She entered her office, grabbed her purse, and pulled out her mulberry lip gloss and compact mirror. As she touched up her lips, she wondered if she should be this excited about going out to lunch with Isaiah and his daughter. Yeah, the man was gorgeous, and he was responsible for a hundred-million-dollar foundation. But he also had baby mama drama, plus unresolved issues with his brother.

Was it really wise to want a relationship with a man who was emotionally unavailable?

Eight

Isaiah was in love, and he was finally ready to admit it to himself. He and Ramona still weren't officially dating. They had spent a lot of time together, though. Over the past month, they had made tremendous progress on his foundation, and Isaiah and Erin had found plenty of occasions to take Ramona to lunch or dinner with them.

Ramona treated Erin like a princess, and her presence was becoming very important to the girl, especially since Tanya had reneged on her promise to pick her up at the end of the month. Tanya had met someone who wanted to take her around the world. The only problem was, her new love didn't want a kid tagging along. So, Tanya had asked if Erin could start the school year with Isaiah. That was fine with him. As a matter of fact, he wanted Erin to begin and end every school year with him, and he had contacted his lawyers to make that happen. He was ready to give Tanya anything she wanted, as long as she would give him full custody of Erin.

Since Isaiah knew what his plans for Erin were, he had to make sure that any woman he got involved with would be willing to become involved with his daughter. And Ramona had more than proven she cared about Erin. So what was he waiting for?

Ramona was beautiful, smart, and funny. Most important, she didn't have a deceitful bone in her body. If he didn't make his move soon, some other guy with sense enough to know a good thing when he saw it would come along and snatch her up. Isaiah realized that he couldn't live with that.

His decision made, Isaiah left his office, walked down the hall, and knocked on Ramona's door.

"Come in," her welcoming voice beckoned.

He opened the door, and a smile lit her face. He knew this woman adored him. He wasn't getting himself involved with another woman who wanted someone else but had settled for what she could get. That wasn't Ramona. Their days would be full of love, laughter, and faithfulness—and, if he had anything to say about it, lots of children. "Hey."

"Hey, yourself."

Still a bit gun-shy, he slowly approached her desk and began with a safe subject. "I just received confirmation that my father will be able to attend our meeting next week."

"Now I'm getting nervous."

"No need to be nervous. You've done all the work. We've pretty much decided on which organizations we want to support; now we just need to present the information to my father."

"Yes, but your father is *the* Joel Morrison," Ramona said with awe in her voice.

Isaiah laughed. "What are you, a throwback groupie from the sixties? You weren't even born when my father was lighting up the big screen."

"But I do have a mother and a grandmother, and both of them loved your father's films. My grandmother has every one of his movies on videocassette, and whenever I'd go there to spend the night, we'd make popcorn and watch a Joel Morrison film."

Isaiah rolled his eyes. "Don't tell him that when you meet him next week. He's pretty grounded these days, and I don't want his head to start swelling."

Ramona shook her head. "Any man who would willingly give away the fortune he worked all his life to acquire would never be in danger of getting a big head over anything."

"You're right—my father is the most humble man I know. I just don't want you gushing over another man," he admitted.

Ramona blushed.

Isaiah immediately felt guilty. "I'm sorry, I wasn't trying to embarrass you." He put his hands in his pockets. "Look, I really came over here because I wanted to invite you to dinner with me and Erin tonight."

"Sounds like a plan. Where are we going?"

"I'll let you and Erin decide. But there's something else you should know."

"What's that?"

"I hired a babysitter for Erin tonight. I'd like for us to have some time alone so we can talk."

"So, what are you saying, Isaiah?" she asked cautiously.

"I'm saying that after dinner, I want to drop Erin off at home and then take you someplace for a cup of coffee…and talk about us."

"I think I'd like that very much."

Again, there was no guile in Ramona's response. Most women he'd met would have tried to play coy—act as if they weren't aware that anything had been transpiring between the two of them over the last couple of months. But not Ramona. She wasn't afraid to let him know that she was feeling him just as much as he was feeling her. He liked that. "I'll pick you up at seven. Is that okay?"

"That's fine."

"Well, until tonight." He walked out of her office, wondering if he was being a fool wasting time on courtship when he really wanted to just go ahead and buy the ring and ask this woman to marry him already. He'd spent less time getting to know Tanya before proposing than he had spent with Ramona. They'd dated less than a month when she had convinced him to marry her. He should have known something was up; nobody falls in love that quick.

Thinking about Ramona again, Isaiah almost retracted his thought on how quickly a person could fall in love. Because the more time he spent with her, the more he felt that she was the woman for him. And he needed to make sure that he could call what he was feeling "love."

~

"Mallory, you'll never believe what just happened!" Ramona skipped over the pleasantries when her cousin answered her cell phone.

"Pastor Isaiah finally asked you on a real date?"

"How did you know?"

"Girl, all I can say is, it's about time. I don't know how you let that man beat around the bush for this long. My goodness, the man may be rich, but he's not the only man in the universe."

"His money has nothing to do with it. I like Isaiah for the man he is, plain and simple."

"I'm just glad that 'the man he is' finally caught a clue."

"Leave him alone, Mallory. Isaiah's been through a lot these past few years."

"Okay, okay, if you like him, then I love him. My mouth is closed from here on out."

"Thanks, girl. Will you be coming straight home from work?"

"Yeah, what's up?"

"I need you to help me pick out the right outfit for tonight."

Since Erin would be with them for part of the evening, Ramona didn't want to wear anything too dressy. They were, after all, going to dinner with an eight-year-old. Mallory had a white dress from Macy's that Ramona had been coveting ever since she'd brought it home. The dress stopped at the knee and was layered in ruffles. It had the slimming effect that every woman wanted, and the color would look really nice with her caramel complexion.

Late that afternoon, Mallory walked out of her closet holding the very item Ramona had wanted so desperately to wear. She grabbed the dress and the matching white shoes out of Mallory's hand and kissed her on the cheek. "Thanks, Cuz. You're one in a million."

"Don't sweat it. The dress will probably look better on you, anyway."

"We both know that's not true, but I love you for trusting me with it. I promise not to spill anything on it."

Mallory sat down on the edge of her bed. "Don't spend all night worrying about spilling something on yourself. What you need to concentrate on is bagging this rich guy. I can't believe this is happening to someone in my family. We normally get the duds of the bunch."

Ramona stood at her cousin's bedroom door; she was anxious to go to her room and get dressed, but she couldn't let Mallory think of Isaiah as just some rich guy she was trying to "bag." She leaned against the door frame. "Actually, Mallory, Isaiah's father is rich. Isaiah has a considerable foundation that he is responsible for, but all of that money will be given away. I'm not sure how much money he really has to his name."

"Trust me, he's got enough. Did you pay attention to those dresses he sent you? Girl, they weren't cheap."

"What I'm trying to say is, it's not the money that attracts me. It's the man. Isaiah is kind, warm, and giving. And I'm just glad that he wants to spend his time with me."

Mallory rolled her eyes heavenward. "Girl, I don't know what side of the family you were born on."

"That's just it. I may have been born to a family who'd rather see the money before the man, but I've also been born again...and

God has helped me to really see the man and let the rest fall where it will."

"Mmph." Mallory smirked.

"What?"

"Nothing, girl. I mean, I'm just saying…you talk a good game. But you still haven't told Pastor Isaiah about Dwayne."

Talk about hitting a person right between the eyes. Since the night Isaiah had informed her that she couldn't know the difficulty of forgiveness, since she'd never been married, she'd been searching for a way to tell him the truth. She hadn't actually lied directly to his face, because she'd never confirmed that she hadn't been married. He'd just assumed as much from the title she'd written on her application.

After a guilty pause, she admitted, "I've been trying to find a way to tell him the truth. But if we are getting ready to begin a relationship, then I have no other choice but to tell him tonight."

Nine

Erin wanted Mexican, so they went to a family-owned restaurant not far from Isaiah's house. The three of them had placed their orders of chicken burritos with rice and beans. A bowl of salsa and chips had been placed on the table. Ramona wanted some of those chips but couldn't take the chance of dripping salsa on her cousin's white dress. Being an observant man, Isaiah noticed that her eyes kept darting toward the chips.

"You know you want some, so why don't you just grab a chip and be done with it?"

"Do you know how many calories are in one of those chips?" Ramona responded, trying to make light of the situation without admitting that she didn't want to spill anything.

"I knew that was the problem." Isaiah picked up a chip, scooped a mound of salsa on it, and held it to her mouth. "You're too skinny to be worried about a few chips. And I may need to fatten you up a bit anyway."

Ramona laughed. "Okay, okay, I'll eat." She bit into the chip.

"That's more like it." After she'd finished the first chip, Isaiah scooped another chip in the salsa, but as he prepared to feed it to her, a dribble of red liquid dripped off and headed south.

Ramona gasped and glanced down. The salsa had splattered one of the ruffles of her dress. "Oh, no," she whimpered.

"I'm so sorry, Ramona." Isaiah grabbed some napkins and attempted to wipe the salsa off before she could stop him. All he did was make the red smudge larger. "I'll fix it, just give me a minute." He left the booth as if their table had just been set on fire.

Ramona dipped her napkin in her water glass and dabbed at the spot.

"My daddy really likes you," Erin said with a hint of amusement in her voice.

Ramona's hand stopped in mid-dab. She put her napkin on the table and looked at Erin. "Are you okay with that?"

Erin shrugged her shoulder. "He seems happy now and not sad like he used to be," she said and then dug into the chips and salsa, seeming to forget about the matter.

Isaiah brought a waitress back with him who swished some kind of solution on a wet rag and then attacked the spot on Ramona's dress. By the time the woman was finished, Ramona was relieved that she couldn't even tell which ruffle had been affected.

"Whew." Isaiah wiped his forehead as he sat back down. "I really need to pay better attention…I have a habit of spilling stuff on you."

Ramona put her hand on his shoulder. "It's okay, Baby—" She stopped herself mid-sentence, realizing what she'd just called her pastor—and boss. She removed her hand from his shoulder and began tapping it on the table. Thankfully, the server picked that moment to bring their dinners.

Before Ramona could grab her fork and pretend the episode had never occurred, Isaiah put his hand over hers. When she turned to face him, he gazed intently into her eyes and said, "I like how that sounds coming from you."

After dinner, it seemed that Isaiah couldn't get Erin home to the babysitter fast enough. He'd arranged for his housekeeper, Mrs. Powers, to watch her for the rest of the evening. After he'd handed her off, he turned around and ran back to his car, opened the door, and jumped in.

"What's the rush?" Ramona asked. "The coffee shop is open until el—"

Isaiah leaned over and captured her words with a hungry, can't-get-enough kiss that seemed to stun him as much as it surprised her. When their lips parted, he told her, "I've been wanting to do that since the day we met."

"You could have fooled me," Ramona said with a shy grin. "I thought you were thinking I was the worst hiring decision you'd ever made and were trying to find a way to fire me."

"I don't know how much experience you have with men, but my actions toward you in the beginning were due to the strong pull I felt between the two of us. I'm sorry if I caused you to doubt your job performance."

Tell him. Ramona felt a strong pull, but at the moment it wasn't coming from Isaiah. She felt as if the Lord was tugging on her heartstrings, telling her it was time to reveal the truth. She put her hand on Isaiah's shoulder. "I need to talk to you about something."

Isaiah turned the key in the ignition and started driving down the street. "Hold that thought, would you? Let's get to the coffee shop, and we can talk to our hearts' content."

They took their coffees and crumb cakes to a little table in the corner. With couples on either side of them, this was as private as this establishment got. Most of the tables and booths were occupied by professional types, with no time for interacting with anything other than their laptops or iPads.

"Even after everything Tanya did to me, I wasn't the one to file for divorce," Isaiah was saying. "I wanted my marriage to work and was willing to give it another try."

Most people would have thought him a fool for making such a statement to a woman he was trying to impress. But Ramona wasn't most people. She recognized the strength of this man.

"I admire that," Ramona said. "Leaving would have been the easy way out, but you wanted to stick to your vows and love her, in spite of the problems. Not a lot of people could do something so selfless."

"You make it sound like I'm some sort of hero." Isaiah shook his head. "That's not it at all. When Tanya asked me for the divorce, I was being groomed for the role of pastor at the church, and to tell you the truth, part of the reason I wanted to stay married to Tanya was to avoid having to explain a divorce to the congregation."

Ramona had also thought about staying in her marriage for fear of what the people in her church would think. And she wanted to share that so badly, but she couldn't—not until she'd told him about Dwayne.

"Your silence is scaring me," Isaiah said.

"To tell you the truth, Isaiah, I still don't know where I stand with you. So, I just want to hear what you have to say."

"I told you over a month ago that I want you in my life," Isaiah told her. "I just needed to get my head on straight. There was so much deception going on in my marriage that it really shook me up. I had a lot of hard feelings toward Tanya."

"Do you still love her?"

Isaiah grinned. "Oh, so now you've got some questions?"

She cocked her head at him. "You could say that the answer to that question is kind of important to me."

He put his hand over hers. "No, I'm not in love with Tanya anymore. I knew it for sure the day she brought Erin to my office. She asked if we could get back together, and I told her that ship had sailed."

Ramona just knew that evil woman had been trying to make a move on Isaiah! That was probably why she'd taken an instant dislike to her—that, and the extortion.

"I knew then that I was free from her, and that God had released me to love again."

Did he say "love"?

He moved his chair a little closer to her and took her hand again. Gazing into her eyes, he said, "I am ready to love again. I think God placed you in my life for a reason. But before we go any further, I have to make sure that you understand what's going on with my family situation." He took a deep breath. "By that, I mean that I've hired an attorney and am fighting for full custody of my daughter. So, how would you feel about being with a man with a ready-made family?"

Ramona opened her mouth to say that she would be honored to be not only a part of his life but Erin's, as well. But then she heard a voice that caused the hair on her neck to stand up.

"Well, well, well. Ramona Verse, what are you doing here?" He sounded like a disgruntled postal worker.

Ramona knew these next few minutes in her life would not be good. She pulled her hand from Isaiah's grasp and looked up at her ex-husband. "How are you doing?" She tried to sound calm, hoping that he would just keep it moving, to Siberia or maybe Libya.

"I'm doing good. Obviously not as good as you, though, since I don't seem to have a girlfriend right now." He glanced pointedly at Isaiah.

"But you do have a bunch of money that doesn't belong to you."

"What's mine is yours, and what's yours is mine, sweetheart."

Isaiah looked from Ramona to Dwayne and then back again. "Am I missing something?" he asked her.

Ramona sent a warning glance in Dwayne's direction, then looked at Isaiah. "You're not missing anything. He was just leaving...isn't that right?"

"I'll leave after you introduce me to your *date*." He said "date" as if the word had rabies.

Not waiting for Ramona, Isaiah stuck out his hand. "I'm Isaiah Morrison. And you are?"

"Oh, nobody important," he said, shaking Isaiah's hand. "Just Dwayne Verse, Ramona's husband."

Ten

R amona's *what?*"

"Her husband."

"My ex-husband," Ramona corrected.

Isaiah stood up. "What's going on here?"

"Ah, my feelings are hurt. You didn't tell your boyfriend about me?" Dwayne said, mocking Ramona.

Ignoring Dwayne, Ramona turned to Isaiah and grabbed his hand. "This is what I wanted to tell you tonight. You got the wrong impression about my singleness. You thought that I hadn't been married before."

Isaiah let go of her hand. "And you sure didn't bother to clear up that misunderstanding, did you?" He looked at her as if she'd just broken his favorite toy. He pulled his car keys out of his pocket. "I need to pick up Erin. I can still take you home—that is, unless your husband wants to take you."

"Ex-husband," Ramona said again as she stood up and walked out behind Isaiah.

"Oh, so you're just going to leave me hanging?" Dwayne hollered.

Isaiah was practically sprinting to the car. Ramona had to grab his arm to halt his steps. When he turned to face her, she said, "Please don't leave me; I want to come with you, but I need to say something to Dwayne really fast."

She turned and stalked back toward the man who had taken so much from her…and still it hadn't been enough. Now he had come after the one good thing Ramona had in her life, and she wasn't about to let him get away with it without telling him just what a parasite he was. Pointing a finger angrily at him, she said, "I just want you to know that you haven't beaten me and you won't make me hate you."

"I don't hate you, either. As a matter of fact, I think I still love you, if you can believe that."

"It doesn't matter what I believe. But what you need to understand is that there is no more you and me." She waved her finger back and forth between them. "I want nothing else to do with you. But I do pray for you. I pray that God will help you come to terms with who you really are, so that, one day, you'll be able to crush the monster that's inside of you."

When he'd walked up to Ramona and Isaiah, he'd been full of arrogance. But the arrogance apparently was slipping as he was faced with a woman who had bothered to pray for him even after all that he'd done to her. "Thank you."

"No need to thank me." She started to walk away from him. But then she turned back and said, "Oh, and I want my money back."

She got in the car with Isaiah. "Thanks for waiting on me."

Isaiah didn't respond. He backed the car out of his parking space and sped down the street.

"Slow down, Isaiah. You don't want to get a speeding ticket just because you're mad at me."

"I just don't understand how you could have lied to me about something as important as this."

"I didn't lie to you—I just didn't correct your assumption."

Instead of dropping his speed, he accelerated. "Really? Is that why you filled out your application and all of the other paperwork as 'Miss' Ramona Verse instead of 'Mrs.'?"

They came up to a red light, and Ramona thanked God that Isaiah had to slow down. "I was still angry about all the stuff Dwayne had done to me, I just wanted to forget all about being married to him. He cheated on me several times and then stole all of my money when I asked for a divorce."

"So, he's the reason you live with your cousin?"

"Yes."

"I thought you were a breath of fresh air, a woman who didn't lie and scheme to get what she wanted. I fell for you because of how honest and guileless you seemed." He shook his head. "Turns out you're just as deceitful as my ex-wife. You're probably still married to the guy! I don't know where my head has been lately, but I'm sure figuring some things out now."

It hurt her to listen while Isaiah accused her of falsehoods. She hadn't meant to mislead him, and she would give almost anything to go back and correct his misunderstanding of her marital status from the start. She should have told him early on about her miserable marriage and the divorce that had followed.

"What gets me," he continued, "is that I've talked to you about my ex-wife and my divorce, and all the while you knew that I had no clue that you had been married, but you never said a word."

She turned and looked out the window. What could she say? He was right. She knew that she should have told him the truth, but she just hadn't been able to pull the words out of her mouth. Tears rolled down her face as she accepted the fact that she had lost Isaiah before she'd ever really had him.

When Isaiah pulled the car to a stop in front of Mallory's house, Ramona turned to him, hoping that she would somehow find the right words to say. But she had nothing.

He looked at her blankly. "Good night, *Mrs.* Verse."

Wiping the tears from her face, Ramona sniffled. "I made a mistake, Isaiah. I should have told you about my ex-husband. But everything else I told you was true."

"Well, thanks for that."

His sarcastic tone undid her. She opened her door and put one foot out before turning back to him. "I told you before, Isaiah: forgiveness is a choice. You seem to think that people have to be perfect to qualify for your mercy and love. But people aren't perfect. We are flawed, emotional creatures who somehow still need love anyway."

Isaiah sat with his father, Joel, his brother Eric, and Ramona in the church conference room, ready to listen to Ramona's presentation on the organizations she was recommending they invest in. She focused mostly on his father and Eric, though her eyes kept darting at Isaiah. He hadn't spoken with her, besides a quick hello or good-bye, since the episode at the coffee shop. She seemed to be doing just fine, for as upset as she'd been when he'd dropped her off.

She handed each of them a portfolio. "I have sent more detailed information on what we're about to discuss to your e-mail addresses for your reference. The information I'm presenting today shows our investment and giving strategy." Setting her own copy of the portfolio in front of her, she cleared her throat. "Please open to the first page."

She reviewed the table of contents with them, guiding them through the documentation so that they would be able to locate whatever information they needed.

"Anyway," she said, "on page five, you'll see all of the investments in our proposed financial portfolio; page eight details the charitable organizations we will be supporting."

The meeting went on for another hour as Ramona talked figures, percentages, and other investment lingo. Isaiah tried to pay attention, but he kept getting distracted by Ramona's fine looks—and by his inner voice, berating him for the immature way he'd reacted to her accidental revelation last weekend. He woke up from his daydream when Ramona started wrapping up the presentation.

"Thank you, gentlemen, for taking the time to review this information."

"This looks really good, Ramona," Isaiah's father said. "I can tell that you poured your heart and soul into this project."

A smile crossed her lips. "Thank you, Mr. Morrison. Coming from you, that is high praise indeed."

Isaiah wasn't ready for the meeting to end. He didn't know the next time he'd have the opportunity to gaze at Ramona for one hour without interruption. So, he tried stalling, keeping his eyes on Ramona as he spoke. "Dad, did I tell you that Ramona's grandmother has all of your old movies?"

She rolled her eyes heavenward, as if to say, *"Give me a break."* "If you have any questions, I'm sure Pastor Isaiah will be able to answer them for you." With that, she stood up and handed Isaiah the folder that she'd had in front of her during the meeting. "Thank you again for your time. Have a good day, everyone." She walked out of the conference room without another word.

⌒

"You've got a good one there, Isaiah," Eric said while flipping through his folder. "You'd better hold on tight to that one."

Isaiah opened the folder that Ramona had handed him before leaving the meeting, and his eyes bugged out. "I can't believe it—she quit," he said before he could stop himself.

"She *what?* But why?" his father asked. "She seems like the perfect person for a job like this."

Dumbfounded, Isaiah could only hand him the folder containing her two-word resignation letter.

Eric took the folder from his father and thumbed through it. "Why did she give you a copy of her divorce decree?"

Isaiah snatched the document away from his brother and scanned it quickly. Ramona was indeed divorced, as she had told him. And he'd accused her of lying about it. Was that why she'd quit, even though she desperately needed this job? It seemed she wanted to get away from him more than she wanted to get her finances back in order. For a financial planner, that was huge. "I'll be right back," Isaiah told his father and brother. Then he rushed out of the room.

He'd messed up, and now he needed to fix it before he lost the woman he was born to love. When he reached Ramona's office, she was standing at her desk, filling a box with photos and little knick-knacks that she'd brought with her. She looked up as he walked in. "Don't worry; I'm not taking anything that doesn't belong to me."

"Why are you leaving?"

She gave him a why-do-you-think? look and continued packing.

He held up his hands. "Look, Ramona, I was mad after your husb—ex-husband confronted us. But if you would have given me some time, I would have gotten over it."

"Oh, really? And how am I supposed to believe that, when you can't even forgive your own brother? I noticed that Shawn was not in attendance today."

She had him there. "You're right that I haven't forgiven Shawn yet. But I'm getting closer and closer to it every day." He stepped nearer to her. "You didn't do anything to me, Ramona. So you don't need my forgiveness. I need to ask you to forgive me."

She paused her packing. "What do I need to forgive you for?"

"For judging you based on my past experiences." He inched even closer. "I should have believed you when you told me that you were indeed divorced. I can't understand why you didn't tell me in the first place."

"I wanted to tell you."

He put his fingers to her lips. "Shh. You don't need to explain anything to me. I trust you, because my heart tells me that I can."

A tear slid down her face.

"You told me that forgiveness is a choice, I agree with you. But you need to know that, for me, love isn't a choice. I can't control my heart, and it wants you."

"But Isaiah—"

He silenced her with a kiss so passionate, so filled with all the love he was feeling, that it swept them away to a land where lies and betrayals don't exist. There was only hope and love for them now. "So, what do you say, Baby?" he asked when they came up for air.

"About what?" She had a dazed look on her face.

"About loving me...having and holding me...from this moment, until death do us part? It's your choice."

"Then I choose you," Ramona told him without hesitation. "Now, Pastor, about that kiss."

"What about it?"

"Let's do it again."

Isaiah was about to oblige his woman, but as he leaned his head forward, he heard someone behind him clear his throat. They both turned, and there stood Isaiah's father and Eric in the doorway.

"Um, I think you need to wait until after the wedding before you kiss her like that again, Son."

Isaiah and Ramona laughed at the wise words of Joel Morrison. But then they began to rejoice, because the preacher's heart had been mended.

The Politician

Prologue

There was never enough vodka in the house. Linda Morrison threw the empty bottle in the trash, then grabbed her purse and keys and stumbled all the way to her silver Lexus. Her daughter, Kivonna, was spending the night with friends, and her husband, Eric, was out saving the world, as usual. Leaving Linda home alone, again.

Linda had learned to occupy her time alone with vodka, popcorn, and movies. Tonight, however, she figured she'd skip the popcorn...too many calories. She backed out of the driveway and swerved, then straightened the wheel and continued driving out of their subdivision. She turned on a narrow side street and wondered for the hundredth time why, with all of the money they paid the city in taxes, there weren't more streetlights on some of the back roads. Her husband was the mayor, so she decided she would ask him about that when he finally showed up at home, sometime later that night.

She suddenly realized, to her shame, that she hadn't changed out of her ratty jean shorts and her too-tight T-shirt in her rush to get more vodka. Being married to the mayor made her the first lady of Cincinnati, and she couldn't come out of the house looking any old way. Even so, Linda never asked Eric how she looked anymore. As long as she'd known the man, she'd never heard him tell a lie; so, unless she wanted to hear about the ill-fitting clothes she wore or the extra weight she'd picked up, she didn't even go there with him. For a woman so flawed, it was hard living with a man so principled and picky. She opened her purse, fished out her comb and lipstick, and pulled down the sun visor, consulting the mirror as she brushed her hair and touched up her lips. A car horn honked.

She closed the visor to see who was honking at her. That's when she realized that she was driving on the wrong side of the street, with another car headed straight toward her. She grabbed hold of the steering wheel with both hands and yanked hard to the right. She lost control, and the car seemed to take on a mind of its own, zigzagging at full speed. At one point, Linda thought she was driving on two wheels rather than four.

"Oh God, help me…help me!" she screamed as her car crashed into the oncoming vehicle.

After the head-on impact, Linda's car swerved and twirled until the passenger side connected with an unyielding pole. The air bag burst forth, stopping her head from hitting the steering wheel…and that was the last thing she remembered.

One

Linda felt her head pounding like African drums as she opened her eyes and looked around. She was in her bed, but she didn't remember going to sleep last night. When did she put on these awful striped pajamas? She pushed the covers off and tried to get up, but her body felt as if she'd been in a train wreck.

She fell back on her pillows and pressed her hand to her head, trying to relieve her killer headache. As her hand skimmed her face, it touched something puffy and swollen. The entire left side of her face felt tender and inflamed. *What happened to me?* "Eric!" she cried in a panic. "Eric!" She glanced around the room, half expecting to see her husband lying facedown on the floor in a pool of blood, like one of those horrible true-crime shows where someone breaks in and beats the husband and wife to death. But she wasn't dead. And Eric wasn't on the floor.

"Eric," she called again.

This time, the bedroom door burst open, and Eric stormed in like a madman...not "mad" as in *crazy*, just mad. "What is it?" he barked.

"What happened to me?" she wailed. "My face is swollen and my body aches all over." *Oh no*, she thought, horrified. *Did Eric come home last night, find me drunk, and beat me?* Things had been bad between them, but had they truly gotten that bad?

"You don't remember what you did last night?" Eric asked, inching toward the bed.

Linda couldn't meet his eyes. She lowered her head as she thought. She knew she had been drinking, and Eric would hate knowing that, but she couldn't remember anything else. She certainly didn't know what she'd done to get all banged up. "Hand me a mirror."

"How about this instead?" He handed her two pills and a glass of water. "You might want to wait a few days before looking in the mirror."

Linda gladly popped the pills in her mouth and gulped the water, wishing her husband could have turned it into wine, like Jesus did. She handed Eric the glass and leaned back against her pillows. Frowning, she asked him, "Did we get in a fight or something?"

Uh-oh. Now he looked like a mad *and* offended black man. His bald head glistened, and his dark brown eyes shone with both fire and ice. Linda had always thought her husband was the sexiest man alive. At six foot three, he towered over her five-foot-seven frame. His broad shoulders and muscular chest used to make her feel so safe and protected...but that was before.

"How could you even say something like that?" he growled. "What would I look like, putting my hands on you?"

She winced. "I didn't mean to upset you, Eric. I just don't understand why I'm so sore and busted up."

"You fell down the stairs," he spat. He sat down on the bed next to her and sighed. "You almost killed yourself, Linda. How do you think Kivonna and I would have felt if we had come home and found you dead?"

"I-I'm sorry."

Eric shook his head. "I just don't understand why you'd rather drink yourself into oblivion than live in the real world with us."

Ignoring the pain, she lifted her hand to his beautiful face. "I'm sorry, Baby. I swear I'll do better."

"I need you alert and in the game with me. My campaign for governor begins in just a few months. I have never wanted anything more than I want to win this election."

And that was the problem. Eric had never wanted *her* as much as he wanted his political career. When they were dating, Linda had thought that she could handle being with such an ambitious man. She'd thought that she could love him enough for the both of them. But that was before she'd married him. Before she'd given birth to one child and suffered three miscarriages. Before she'd started drinking to dull the pain—and sometimes just to get out of bed. Before he'd stopped loving her.

"I'm staying home today, and I'm going to take care of you. Would you like that?" Eric asked as he stood up.

She nodded. *Wow.* Maybe she should fall down the stairs once a month, or maybe just once every other month, if it would get her that kind of attention.

"Let me go check and see if Maria is finished with your breakfast."

"Thanks, Eric. I appreciate what you're doing for me."

After he'd left the room, she realized she hadn't bothered to ask what the breakfast menu looked like. But she probably didn't need to worry. Maria had been both cook and housekeeper for the past five years, and Linda loved everything the woman prepared. She had even been jealous at times of how much Eric seemed to love Maria's food. Linda never failed to notice the smiles he sent her and the moans that escaped his lips when he feasted on a meal she'd prepared. Those smiles and moans never showed up when Maria was off and Linda had to cook.

"Stop it," she chided herself. "Stop being such a baby about everything." Before marrying Eric, she had been vibrant and full of life. She'd been a cheerleader in both high school and college; she'd been picked as prom queen and voted the biggest flirt on campus. Fun had been her middle name.

Eric had always been so serious, so strictly business, and Linda had thought he needed someone like her in his life. With a handsome face, a sexy smile, and a father who had several hundred bazillion dollars in the bank, Eric could've had any woman he wanted. Linda had been determined to win his heart by proving that she could be an asset to him. As it turned out, she'd become an embarrassment to him.

She'd gotten the man she wanted, all right; now she had to live with him. Throwing back the covers, Linda scooted to the edge of the bed. The blinds were open, and the sunlight coming through was wreaking havoc on her left eye. She made her way across the room with baby steps, stopping often for deep breaths. When she finally reached the window, she touched the control panel to close the blinds but stopped when a reflective surface in the driveway caught her eye. She pressed her face to the window and almost fainted at the sight of her car. The front was completely destroyed, the windshield shattered.

Her bedroom door opened, and she turned around, knees wobbling beneath her. Eric set her breakfast tray on the dresser and ran over to her. "What are you doing up?" He picked her up and carried her back to the bed, then rushed back over to the window and closed the blinds.

"What happened to my car?" she finally managed.

Two

Eric carried the tray over to the bed and lowered himself down next to her.

"Did you hear me, Eric?" Linda sat up. "I asked you what happened to my car."

He just sat there with a dumbfounded expression on his face. "You really don't remember a thing about last night, do you?"

She turned away from him. What did he want her to do, admit that she was a falling-down drunk who now suffered from blackouts? She couldn't do that. Maybe there was another explanation for her memory loss. She rubbed her forehead—the side that wasn't throbbing. "Maybe I need to see a doctor. I mean, I'm surprised that a tumble down our carpeted stairs could jack me up this much, and with this memory loss...."

He set the tray of food in front of her. "I think it looks worse than it really is. You just need to eat and get some rest. If you're not feeling better in a day or two, then I'll make a doctor's appointment for you. Okay?"

She grabbed a piece a bacon from her plate. "Okay."

"Now, about your car...."

Linda took a bite of scrambled eggs and looked over at him. He appeared to hesitate for a moment, but before she could wonder too much about that, he opened his mouth again.

"Michael was in an accident last night."

"Michael who?"

"Michael Underwood, our gardener. You sent him to the store to get something for you."

Linda had been home alone yesterday, so if she had followed her normal pattern, the only thing she would have wanted would have been something to drink. Would she really have sent Michael for some wine or vodka? "I must have really been messed up last night."

The anger returned to his eyes. "Yeah, you were."

Linda pushed the tray away. "I don't want to argue with you, Eric. I know I messed up. Just let me get some sleep and we can talk about this later."

Eric stood up. "What am I supposed to tell Kivonna when she gets home from school and wants to see you?"

"Just tell her that I'm not feeling well. She'll understand that Mommy needs her rest."

He jammed his hands in his pockets. "She's heard that enough to know exactly what it means."

"Please, Eric. I really don't feel good right now." She lowered her head to the pillow and pointed at the tray. "Can you just take that back downstairs? Maybe I'll eat some more later."

He didn't respond; he just grabbed the tray and left the room.

Wallowing in self-pity, Linda wondered just how long she and Eric could go on like this. They used to dance together; she used to be able to make him laugh. Now she lived in fear of the day Eric would deem her a liability to his career goals. He probably would have divorced her years ago if it weren't for the fact that voters tended to look unfavorably on divorced candidates, especially when said candidate had been the one to pull the plug on the marriage.

Linda needed a drink. She closed her eyes and tried to will away the thought. All of her problems with Eric had begun the day she started finding comfort in a bottle. She wanted to change, but she was powerless to stop her lust for the drink. Maybe if she slept, she would wake up with her mind set on something other than her need for alcohol. As she drifted off to sleep, something big and white burst in her face, and she dreamed of lying on a cushiony cloud.

She tossed and turned awhile, finally giving up on the idea of getting any more sleep for now. Then she grabbed the TV remote and checked the local news channel. The anchor was talking about a murder that had occurred the night before. Linda was about to change the channel when a picture of a crumpled car that looked a lot like her silver Lexus came into view.

She turned the volume up. A photo of another car appeared on the screen, and it looked as if the Jaws of Life had been used on it. She didn't envy whoever had been in that car. The television camera flashed to a hospital, with a reporter standing outside. "The City of Cincinnati is collectively holding its breath, praying that Terrell Anderson will pull through surgery and be able to play ball again."

Terrell Anderson? She knew that name. He was supposed to be the great hope of Ohio. When Lebron James left Cleveland, every professional sports team in Ohio—be it basketball, baseball, football, or hockey—began looking for the next superstar. Someone the people could brag on and say, "He's one of us, and proud of it!" Terrell Anderson had been the one.

Terrell was unstoppable on the field. Dubbed "The Touchdown Kid," he had just been recruited by the Cincinnati Bengals. It wasn't just the people of Cincinnati who were happy about the draft pick; all of Ohio had stood up and cheered. It was as if the entire state had reclaimed some of its dignity when Terrell signed with the Bengals. And with the economy having bottomed out, manufacturing jobs leaving right and left—not to mention Lebron cutting and running—Ohio needed this boost.

But now it appeared as if one car accident had done what a field full of running backs couldn't. Terrell had been knocked out of the game, and as the news reporter interviewed several passersby about the tragedy, one person after the next seemed to say the same thing: "Man, he's got to recover. The game won't be the same without 'The Touchdown Kid.'"

The anchor appeared on the screen again, and Linda held her breath as he said, "Mayor Eric Morrison has got to be shaking in his boots this morning. It appears that the car that hit Terrell belonged to his wife, Linda Morrison, but had been driven by the gardener who was out on an errand."

Linda clasped her hand over her mouth. What had she done? Eric had to be mortified. And poor Michael! Eric would fire the man, even though she had been the one to send him on the errand that had caused the accident. She would have to convince Eric to let him keep his job.

And what about Terrell Anderson? There had to be something that they could do to help the young man. She just prayed that he would pull through surgery all right.

⌒

"Mayor Morrison, we've got trouble," Michael Underwood said as he came into the kitchen.

"What kind of trouble?"

He nodded toward the front window. "So far, it looks like Channel Two, Twenty-two, and Seven are all outside, with camera crews and everything."

Eric rushed to the window and looked out. Camera crews had been sighted at his house a time or two before, such as when some of the city workers had gone on strike and wanted the mayor to step in and broker a fair deal for them. Eric had worked from home for two days, trying to avoid the media, while he came up with a solution, but the paparazzi had found him anyway.

Another time the media had showed up at his doorstep had been right after a heinous murder in the downtown area. Before Eric could get dressed and down to City Hall the morning after, the reporters were ringing his doorbell and wanting to know what he was going to do about all the crime in the city.

Both of those meetings with the press had been grueling, and both had been significant challenges to his political career. However, Eric would rather face reporters on either of those issues again than the issue that had brought them to his house today.

He turned to Michael. "Stay inside; let me handle this." Then, taking a deep breath, he walked to the foyer, opened the front door, and marched toward his lion's den. The sharp-fanged creatures were waiting to devour him, but he was determined not to let that happen. He'd worked so hard for this city, year after year, plugging away, making communities safer, bringing more businesses to the region. It was his turn to run for governor now, and he would not let this incident stand in his way—not even if he had to lie, bribe, and transact underhanded deals to make the situation go away. He put on a bright smile as he came face-to-face with the press. "Hello, everyone. What brings you out to my home this lovely afternoon?"

Microphones were shoved into Eric's face. He stepped back.

"We have received reports that a man employed by you drove the car that hit Terrell Anderson last night."

Another reporter said, "The car is registered in your wife's name."

Still another reporter said, "Terrell just came out of surgery."

Eric lifted his hands. "Hold up. Is there a question in there somewhere?"

"Why was your gardener driving your wife's car?"

Calmly, he said, "My wife had fallen down the stairs. I was at work, so she asked Michael to run to the store and get her some pain medication."

"Why didn't he take his own car?"

"I don't know; I wasn't here at the time," Eric responded.

"Where is Mr. Underwood now?" one of the reporters hollered out.

"Where is Mrs. Morrison?" another asked.

"Why does that matter? My wife has nothing to do with—"

"It was her car," someone shouted, cutting him off.

"Mayor Morrison, are you aware that Terrell Anderson may never be able to play football again?"

Eric frowned in genuine anguish. "I am very sorry to hear that about Mr. Anderson. My hope is that his surgery and rehabilitation will be enough to get him back on his feet and on the field again." With that, he turned, strode back into his house, and closed the door without answering another question.

"Do you think they bought it?" Michael asked him.

"I don't know, but I need to get you out of here. What time of year do you and your family normally go on vacation?"

Michael shook his head. "We've got five kids, and never have enough money to take them anywhere. We barely have enough to stay in our home."

"What are you talking about? I just gave you fifty thousand dollars."

"And I thank you for that money, Mr. Morrison, but I'm putting that toward college for my children."

"Okay, well, spend the night here tonight, but call your wife and tell her to pack some bags for you and the kids. I'm going to pay for a weeklong trip to Disney World for all of you." Without waiting for a response, Eric walked out of the room, his mind completely focused on putting out this fire that his wife had set.

Three

A scorpion was coming after her. Linda leaned back, but no matter how far she pulled away, it kept moving in. She screamed and was jolted out of her nightmare.

She looked at the clock on her nightstand. It was five thirty in the evening. The nightly news would be on, so she turned on the TV and clicked to one of the local news stations. They weren't talking about anything but the weather, so she changed the channel. Eric was on television. He appeared to be in front of their house. But what struck Linda as odd was the fact that he had just told a reporter that Michael Underwood had driven her car to get her medication after she'd fallen down the stairs.

At the moment, she felt as if a bus had run over her, so she knew she would have been in even more pain last night. Why would Michael have left her to go to the store for pain medicine, when she had a medicine cabinet full of painkillers in the master bathroom? That just didn't make sense. Something was up, and she was going to get to the bottom of it.

Her bedroom door opened, and she changed the channel.

Eric popped his head in. "You're awake. How are you feeling?"

"A little better. I think I want to get up and walk around."

"I'd rather that you stay in bed. Isaiah's wedding is this weekend, and I really need you to be in top form for that."

"What if my face is still swollen? Will you take me, or will you leave me at home, like you did when you went to celebrate Elaine's birthday with your family?"

He stepped into the room, closed the door, and sat down on the bed next to her. "You were drunk when I came home to get you. There was no way that you would have been able to get on a plane in that condition. And to be truthful, I would have been mortified to take you anywhere."

"Poor Eric. You got the short end of the stick when you married me, didn't you?"

"Your words, not mine."

But he hadn't bothered to deny them, and that's what hurt her the most. Her husband didn't love her anymore, but she had never forgotten what their love had felt like when it was new. For her, it had been powerful enough to sustain her through the years that hadn't been so great for them. But it was hard to be in love alone. "Okay, Eric. I'll stay in bed for the rest of the evening. Can you just bring me some soup or something?"

"Coming right up." He jumped off the bed as if he couldn't wait to get away from her.

The next morning, after Eric left for the office, Linda made her way down to the kitchen. Every step she took on the stairs was fraught with pain, but the shaking was even worse. She put a pot of coffee on, grabbed an oversized mug, and then searched through her spice cabinet for two bottles of olive oil she'd purchased a year ago. She emptied the bottles, gave them a good cleaning, and then filled them: one with brandy, the other with gin.

Next, she filled her coffee mug halfway with brandy, and then, when the coffee was ready, she topped off the mug. She took a sip. "Aah."

She thought about fixing herself some breakfast, but then she remembered that Maria would be arriving in a few minutes. She'd let her fix her some breakfast. Right now, she just wanted to get back to bed and drink her spiked coffee. She went to return the olive oil bottles to the cabinet, but then she decided that she did not want to have to travel all the way back downstairs for her next fix, so she slid the bottles inside the pockets of her bathrobe. As she was headed out of the kitchen, the back door opened, and Michael walked in.

"Hey, Mrs. Morrison," he greeted her. "I didn't think you'd be out of bed this morning."

She lifted her coffee mug. "Blame it on my obsession with coffee. I'm on my way back upstairs now. Can you please tell Maria that I don't have a preference for breakfast this morning? She can fix anything she'd like to make."

"Sure thing, Mrs. Morrison. I'll make sure she brings your breakfast up as soon as it's out of the skillet."

"Thanks, Michael." She turned, ready to escape with her special brew, but then she remembered the accident and knew that she couldn't just let it go unacknowledged. "Uh, Michael? I wanted to apologize for sending you out the other night. I'm sure you must be pretty banged up from that car accident."

He lifted his right arm and touched his left shoulder, rubbing it. "I banged my shoulder up pretty bad, but I'll heal; don't you worry about me."

Linda shook her head. "Funny thing is, I look more like I've been in a car wreck than you do." She laughed at the notion.

As she did so, Michael stopped rubbing his shoulder, but his hand remained there, as if it was stuck. That's when she was reminded of something—the scorpion she'd seen in her dream. Michael's seventeen-year-old son had a scorpion tattooed on the back of his hand. She'd noticed it when his son had helped out with the gardening a time a two.

He saw her looking at his hand and removed it from his shoulder.

She frowned. "You know, Michael, what I don't understand about all of this is, if I fell down the stairs and got this banged up, why would I ask you to go to the store to get pain pills, when I have a bunch of them in my medicine cabinet?"

He shrugged his shoulders. "Maybe you forgot you had those pills or something."

"Mmph. Why didn't you drive your own car to the store?"

"I guess I was so worried about you, I wasn't thinking clearly, either." He looked away from her.

"Have you gotten a lot of flack for hitting Terrell Anderson?"

He shrugged again, not meeting her eyes. "Some people have made a few scathing remarks, but the police cleared me. I lost control of the car. They took a breathalyzer test that night, so they knew that I hadn't been drinking."

Linda looked down at her cup. Driving while under the influence of alcohol would be a serious problem. If she had been the one in the car that night, the police would have arrested her on the spot. She looked back up at him. "I'm sorry I caused you all this trouble."

For the rest of the day, Linda drifted in and out of consciousness. After breakfast, she took several pain pills in order to numb herself, and ended up sleeping more than she wanted to. She tossed and turned, and then a hand reached out to her. It lifted her head off of the fluffy white cloud she had been lying on. The hand belonged to a man who lifted her into his arms and carried her from her car. Linda looked at the hand. She saw a scorpion tattoo.

The next thing she knew, she'd been placed in another car that was driving away. She was reclining in the front passenger seat, and just before closing her eyes and drifting off to sleep, she saw another car. It was black with tinted windows, but what surprised her about the car was that it wasn't flat to the ground; two of the wheels were suspended in the air.

Linda's eyes popped open as she sat up in bed. She looked around, trying to get her bearings. "Was I in an accident?"

When Eric came home from work, Linda told him about her dream and the scorpion tattoo. But Eric brushed her off, saying it was the medication talking, and she just needed to get some more sleep.

By the next morning, she was a little groggy but feeling well rested. She watched Eric as he dressed for work, wanting desperately to talk to him but knowing she couldn't. There simply wasn't anything to say—there was no truth left between them. "Have a nice day," she said as he walked out of the bedroom.

He mumbled something about driving Kivonna to school.

You go ahead, Mr. Mayor, because I'm going to find out—today— exactly what happened to me. She waited in bed until she heard his car pull out of the driveway, then threw the covers back and got out of bed. She was surprised to discover that her body didn't ache as badly as it had for the past few days. Early on, she had wondered if Eric had done her a disservice by not taking her to the hospital. She understood now why he hadn't. No doctor would have believed his cockamamie story about her falling down the stairs—not with how bruised she had been, and not with her crushed and mangled car playing a starring role on the nightly news as the vehicle that very well may have destroyed Terrell Anderson's promising football career.

She went downstairs and headed out back to search for Michael Underwood. Only he had the answers she sought, and today, she was determined to get the man to tell her the truth. But Michael was nowhere to be found. She walked back inside by way of the kitchen door and found Maria at the stove, making breakfast. "Good morning, Maria."

Maria turned. "Good morning, Mrs. Morrison. You look like you're feeling a little better."

Linda touched her face and noticed that the swelling had gone down. She nodded. "Some of the pain is gone. I actually think I'm going to live."

Maria smiled.

"Have you seen Michael?" Linda asked. "I need to ask him a few questions."

Maria shook her head. "Michael's on vacation. Mr. Morrison told him to get on out of here and go enjoy Florida with his family."

How convenient. "So, my husband sent Michael on a vacation, huh?"

A worried look crossed Maria's face. "I thought you knew about it. I'm sure Mr. Morrison will tell you all the details."

"I'm sure he will. I've been sleeping a lot lately, so Eric really hasn't had a chance to talk to me about much of anything."

Maria smiled again, obviously relieved.

"Well, I guess I'll just talk to Michael when he gets back from vacation."

Looking alarmed again, Maria shook her head. "Oh no, ma'am. Michael won't be coming back here. Mr. Morrison gave him a promotion. He'll be overseeing all of the city's landscaping projects."

Isn't that nice for Michael. But this information from Maria only escalated Linda's suspicions. Her husband would never reward an employee for wrecking her car by sending him on vacation and also promoting him. If the accident had really been Michael's fault, Eric would have fired him without a second's hesitation.

Linda still didn't fully remember everything that happened that night, but she did remember that Michael's son—the one with the scorpion tattoo—had been working with him the night of the accident. And she knew what her dream had been showing her: Michael's son had carried her to his car and had driven her back home after the accident. Michael had then stayed at the scene of the crime—and had taken the blame in her place.

As she headed back to her room, tears were streaming down her face. She had been driving drunk and had almost killed someone. As she sat down on her bed, her mind's eye pictured the other car that had been on the road that night. It was leaning on two of its wheels; the other two were in the air. She gasped. "I'm so sorry, Terrell."

At that moment, she knew what she had to do. She jumped in the shower, got dressed in a pair of jeans and a knit sweater, and called for a cab. Linda was going to the hospital to see Terrell Anderson and beg for his forgiveness.

Four

Linda worried herself sick all the way to the ICU. If Eric was trying to hide the fact that she had been driving the car that had caused the accident, he would not want her to visit Terrell Anderson. The swelling in her face might have gone down, but she was still pretty bruised up. What if Terrell had seen her before the car struck him? He might remember what had actually happened that night and notify the police before she had a chance to explain.

Things were bad enough already between her and Eric. How would their marriage ever survive her being arrested while he was in the midst of preparing to run for governor? Tempted to cut and run, Linda latched on to her sense of rightness. If she had indeed hit Terrell while she was driving drunk, the least she could do was face the young man and apologize for her wrongdoing.

She walked down the hall, knowing in her heart that every step she took was creating a bigger rift in her marriage. But, as she looked at the woman standing behind the reception desk at the ICU, Linda felt, deep within, that this moment was bigger than her and Eric. She steadied herself. "I'm here to see Terrell Anderson," she said.

The woman pointed to the waiting room full of people. "Honey, you and everybody else in this city. And I have to tell you the same thing I told most of them: ICU is for immediate family only. You're welcome to sit with the family in the waiting area, but you won't get behind these doors unless his mother or father takes you in to see him."

Linda had never used her position as first lady of Cincinnati to her advantage. She was normally so fearful of embarrassing Eric in public that she kept her mouth shut and just hoped that no one recognized her. But today, she was on a mission; she needed to get behind those double doors. She leaned closer to the woman and said, "I'm Linda Morrison, Mayor Eric Morrison's wife. My gardener was driving the car that struck Mr. Anderson, and I just wanted to check on the young man." Linda hated lying, but there was no way she was going to tell this woman, and everyone in the waiting room, what she believed had really happened. She was remorseful, but she wasn't suicidal.

The woman eyed her warily. "You would think your gardener would be here trying to find out how Mr. Anderson is doing. As far as I know, he hasn't been here yet." Her tone was more than slightly accusatory.

"He's very remorseful," Linda assured her. "The fact that he has harmed someone is tearing him up inside." If she replaced "he" and "him" with "she" and "her," referring to herself, she would be telling the whole truth and nothing but the truth. "So, I decided to come and check on Mr. Anderson myself. Michael was driving my car when it happened, after all."

"Are you the mayor's wife?" asked a youthful male voice from behind Linda.

She turned around and came face-to-face with a young man with cornrows who wore a Cincinnati Bengals jersey and held a football. The young man looked to be about sixteen or seventeen, so Linda knew he didn't play for the Bengals. He was either a fan of Terrell's or one of his family members. "Yes, I'm Linda Morrison."

He held out his hand. "I'm Les Anderson. Terrell is my big brother."

Linda shook his hand. "How is he doing?"

"Not too good, ma'am. He's busted up pretty bad. But Terrell's a fighter. He's not about to lose his contract over some dumb car accident."

"The mayor and I are praying for him," she lied. She and Eric hadn't prayed together—or separately—in years.

"Why don't you sit down with us?" Les asked. "My mom and dad are in the room with Terrell and his doctors right now. I know they would love to see you."

Could she really face Terrell's parents? "I, uh, don't want to intrude."

"You're not intruding. My mom said just this morning that she was surprised the mayor hadn't come to see Terrell, being as how Terrell is so important to this city. But he sent you, right?"

Linda nodded, then followed Les into the waiting area and took a seat next to a young woman with a protruding belly.

Les made the introductions. "Tawanda, this is the mayor's wife, Mrs. Morrison." He turned back to Linda. "This is my brother's fiancée. They're getting married next month."

"That's if he's out of the hospital by then," Tawanda said with tears in her eyes.

"Girl, quit that crying," Les commanded her. "If he's not out of the hospital, you'll just bring that preacher up in here and we'll have a big old party in one of the waiting areas."

Tawanda chuckled, but the look on her face became serious again as she addressed Linda. "A lot of these people think I got pregnant on purpose, just so I could trap me a professional football player. But I love Terrell, and I would marry him today if he would stay awake long enough to say 'I do.'"

"They have him heavily sedated right now?" Linda asked.

"Yeah. I've asked his mom to take away that morphine pump and just let the nurse medicate him every few hours, but she won't listen to me." Tawanda shook her head. "I just don't want my man addicted to nothing but me...you feel me?"

Her comment struck Linda, because she was addicted to more than just her husband. "Yeah, I feel you."

The ICU doors opened, and Linda watched a couple exit, the man practically having to carry the woman, who staggered out, tears streaming down her face. Les and Tawanda both jumped up and hurried to them.

"What's wrong?" Tawanda demanded. "What happened?"

The man waved them off. "Melinda is just overwrought with worry. Terrell is doing fine, just fine."

"Then why is she crying, Dad?" Les asked.

"She's just upset about what the doctors had to say about Terrell's rehab."

"What are they saying?" Tawanda asked, hands pressed to her abdomen.

Terrell's mother spoke now. "The hospital rehabilitation program isn't going to work for Terrell. He needs a sports rehab program, and our insurance won't cover it." With those words, her jaw clenched, and she did a backward kick, banging her foot against the wall behind her.

"Now calm down, Melinda," her husband pleaded. "God will make a way for our boy. We'll get that rehabilitation specialist the doctor told us about."

"How, Fred? You got a quarter of a million dollars? 'Cause I sure don't."

"God will make a way," Fred said again, with conviction.

"The mayor's wife is here, Mama," Les said quietly. "Maybe she can help...get a telethon or something going for Terrell."

Melinda's eyes flashed as she searched the room. Linda stood. "Hello, Mrs. Anderson. I'm very sorry. I know this must be devastating for your family."

"That no-good gardener of yours hasn't even had the decency to show his face at this hospital," Melinda spat, with venom in her voice. "The police cleared him of the accident, but I never will. He has destroyed my son's future."

Condemnation weighed heavily on Linda as she came face-to-face with the woman's pain. "Again, I am sorry for everything your family is going through. I'd like to help if I can."

"You want to help us, then you get my boy to that rehabilitation clinic that can save his career," Melinda demanded. "And you do it now."

⌇

"I'm not going to sugarcoat this for you, Mr. Mayor. Your family is going to be a problem for you in this election," Darien Jones, Eric's campaign manager, told him flatly.

Eric leaned back in his seat. They'd had this conversation too many times. What did Darien want him to do, change families? "Look, Darien, I know my family can be a bit out of control at times, but they mean well."

"A *bit* out of control?" Darien guffawed. "I would love to put Dee Dee and Shawn out there on the campaign trail for you. Come on—a movie star and a football hero are a dream come true for a gubernatorial candidate. But Dee Dee is on marriage number four, and Shawn just got hit with another paternity suit."

That got Eric's attention. He sat up. "He *what*? There's no way."

"Believe it, man. And this one is some video vixen/porn star. Honestly, if you and I didn't go way back, I wouldn't believe that you, Shawn, and Isaiah were distant cousins, let alone blood brothers."

"Hey, now. What's Isaiah got to do with this?"

Darien lifted his arms and then let them flop back down. "Isaiah might not be involved in a bunch of messy situations like your other two wonderful siblings, but he could end up hurting your chances of being governor anyway."

"How so?"

"Those messages he preaches—he's all fire and brimstone: 'Serve Jesus or go to hell.' And I got to tell you, Eric, the general public just doesn't feel that kind of stuff anymore."

"Just because people don't want to hear it doesn't change the truth of the gospel. At least, that's what Isaiah and my dad have always told me." Eric didn't exactly know what he believed, but he wasn't about to call his father or brother a liar.

"Yeah, but Eric, the problem is that you've attended his church."

"On occasion." Eric shrugged his shoulders. "I still don't see the problem."

"Let me just say, Barack Obama and Jeremiah Wright."

Eric rolled his eyes. "My brother isn't preaching Black Power; he's preaching about the love of God and the need for salvation."

"It's still a controversial message. All I'm asking you to do is stay away from his church until after the election."

"Isaiah is getting married tomorrow. Is it all right if I attend my brother's wedding? I am the best man, after all."

"Of course you can attend the wedding. It's going to be at your father's ranch—far away from Isaiah's church."

Eric clasped his hands together. "Anything else, Mr. Campaign Manager?"

Darien sat down in the chair next to Eric's desk. They'd been best friends since college, so Darien knew what Eric's kryptonite was, and Eric could tell that he was about to lay it on the line.

Darien folded his arms on the desk and looked Eric straight in the eye. "You've got to do something about Linda's drinking."

Eric was the first to break eye contact. His and Linda's problems were private; he didn't discuss them with family or friends. He'd tried to hide her drinking from everyone, mostly because he felt as if he'd made a huge mistake in marrying her. He had planned his life out from start to finish; he'd known from the time he'd learned to tie his shoes that he wanted to be in politics. He'd also known that he would need a strong woman by his side. His siblings, as messed up as they were, couldn't hurt him as much as Linda. She was the weak link.

As he turned back to his friend, he admitted something that he'd been thinking about for quite some time. "I've been wondering what my chances of getting elected would be if I divorced Linda."

Five

The wedding was spectacular. Ramona had done everything right, from the colorful flower arrangements strewn all over the house to the expertly manicured garden area where the wedding took place to the harpist and the pianist providing music for the ceremony.

Everything was beautiful, but as the bride and groom prepared to say their vows, Linda couldn't enjoy any of it. The night before, after putting Kivonna to bed in the guest suite at Joel Morrison's ranch, she'd told Eric about her trip to the hospital to check on Terrell Anderson.

Eric had exploded. "How dare you go behind my back and do something so destructive!"

"How is visiting a sick person destructive, Eric?" she'd demanded. "You used to beg me to do hospital visits."

"This is different." He'd sat down on the bed and begun taking off his shoes.

"How is it different, Eric? Are you afraid that Terrell will realize that I'm the one who ran into his car and that Michael had nothing to do with it?"

The shoe had fallen from Eric's hand as he'd turned to face her. "I thought you had no memory of that night."

"I still don't remember the actual accident, but I have visions of being pulled out of my car. I think Michael's son must have pulled me out, because I remember seeing that scorpion tattoo on his hand."

Eric hadn't responded, so she'd continued on. "The only thing I can come up with is that Michael noticed that I...uh...wasn't myself, and he and his son must have followed me when I left the house. Then, after the accident, he had his son bring me back home, while he stayed and took the blame for what I did. Am I right?"

His shoulders had slumped as he'd nodded.

"Why did you lie to me, Eric?"

He'd jumped up from the bed and sent her a glare that had shaken her to the core of her being. "Because I was scared, all right?" he'd screamed. "What you did could very well ruin me. But do you care?"

"Of course I care. How can you even doubt it?"

The look he'd given her said that he doubted everything about her.

"Okay, I don't want to argue with you. I just want us to help Terrell Anderson."

"What are you talking about?"

"I want to pay for his rehabilitation."

"Are you crazy?"

Kivonna had burst into the bedroom then. "Daddy, Mommy, what's wrong?"

Linda's muscles had been sore from the activities of the day, so she hadn't gotten up, but she'd held out her arms to Kivonna.

Ignoring her, Kivonna had run to Eric. "What happened, Daddy? Why are you so angry?"

"Daddy's not angry, Hon." He'd patted her on the back. "Now, go on back to bed, and let me talk to your mom."

"Are you sure you're all right?" Kivonna had persisted.

"Yes, Pumpkin." He'd kissed her forehead and then turned her around. "Go on back to bed."

Kivonna had walked out of the room, but not before giving Linda a glare that said, *You're always doing something wrong.* The simple act had brought tears to Linda's eyes. She'd wiped them away and turned back to her husband, knowing she didn't have time to feel sorry for herself. Terrell Anderson needed her to do the right thing, so that he could provide for his family. "I think that paying for Terrell's rehabilitation is the least we can do," she'd said to Eric. "After all, if I hadn't hit him, he would be cashing in on a fifteen-million-dollar contract, rather than worrying that he won't see a dime of that money."

"Don't you see"—Eric had lowered his voice—"that if we do anything for Terrell, some reporter or other busybody might figure out that Michael wasn't the one who hit him? And that the reason Michael had to cover for you is because you're a drunk?"

His words, even though they'd been spoken softly, reasonably, had been like a slap to her face. But, again, Linda had resisted the feel-sorry-blues she normally succumbed to. "I can't just stand by and watch his dreams go up in flames."

"Why not? Every day you choose that bottle over your family, you destroy my dreams. Why can't you destroy Terrell Anderson's dreams, as well?"

The verbal blows had just kept coming, but Linda had determined to bob and weave until she'd gotten her point across. "It's the right thing to do, Eric. If Terrell doesn't receive the right kind of rehabilitation, he may never be able to play football again. I can't live with that. Can you?"

He'd walked toward her, his upper lip curled in disgust, as if he'd eaten some bad calves' liver and chased it down with sour milk. Standing inches from her, he'd said, "What I can't live with anymore is you."

"You don't mean that."

"I do mean it, Linda." Holding his index finger and thumb less than a centimeter apart, he'd told her, "I'm this close to calling a divorce attorney and putting an end to my misery." Then he'd grabbed his pillow off the bed. "I'm sleeping in a separate room from now on."

And now they were at a beautiful wedding, with Eric standing next to his brother, looking just as handsome as he had on their wedding day. But the light had gone out of his eyes, as if he didn't believe in love, joy, or happiness anymore. *Am I to blame for this?* Linda couldn't help but wonder. *Did I suck all the joy and happiness out of him?*

"Hey," her sister-in-law Dee Dee hissed at her, "this is a wedding—you're supposed to at least pretend you believe the bride and groom are headed for their happily ever after."

Dee Dee had never shown her a minute's worth of kindness, and she wanted to tell her to mind her own business. But when she opened her mouth, her words got tripped up on her tears.

"I know that look, honey," Dee Dee said. "I've been there three times before." She grabbed Linda's hand and started to pull her from her seat. "Come with me."

Linda resisted. "B-but we can't get up in the middle of the wedding."

"All that's left is for them to say 'I do.' They'll never miss us."

Linda followed Dee Dee into the house and down a hallway to a secluded room. Dee Dee turned and hugged her. "I hate to see you in pain like this. Is there anything I can do to help?"

Linda was shocked. This was the first time Dee Dee had ever seemed to care about the things that concerned her. In fact, in the ten years that she and Eric had been married, it was the first time Dee Dee had appeared to care about anybody but herself. Touched by her sister-in-law's concern, Linda opened up and told her everything that was going on.

"Wow," was all that Dee Dee said when Linda had finished.

"Tell me about it. And all I asked was that we pay for Terrell's rehabilitation, and your brother threatened to divorce me."

"He didn't mean it, Linda. Eric is one of the straightest arrows I know, so he's probably feeling bad about lying in the first place."

"I admit I was shocked that Eric lied to me about the accident. As long as I've known him, I've never had a reason to doubt anything he told me." Linda closed her eyes for a moment, then opened them again. "I think it's the lying that has caused him to hate me."

Dee Dee waved that suggestion away. "He doesn't hate you. I still remember how much Eric loved you when you two first married. The boy was so giddy, running around like he had a high school crush or something. I knew he had fallen in love even before I saw the two of you together. But the day he brought you home confirmed everything. It was in his eyes, as he followed you from room to room. That kind of love doesn't just go away."

Linda tried to smile. "I hope you're right, because, even after all we've been through, I still love that man. But that doesn't change the fact that I need to help Terrell."

Later on, during the reception, Dee Dee grabbed Linda's arm and whispered in her ear, "I figured out a way to get Terrell Anderson the rehab he needs without involving Eric."

"Really? How?"

"We're going to ask Daddy for the money."

Linda held back. She had done so much damage to her reputation that she couldn't bear to see disappointment in the eyes of one more member of the Morrison family. She shook her head. "I can't tell him what I did. He'll hate me for destroying his son's dreams." Wasn't that what Eric had told her—that she'd destroyed his dreams?

Dee Dee rolled her eyes. "Please. If my father could love me after all the things I put him through, there is no way he'll turn his back on you in your time of need."

"I don't know...."

"You want to help Terrell Anderson, don't you?"

Linda nodded. She had thought of nothing but her own heartache for far too long. The Anderson family needed her to be strong. "Okay," she finally conceded, "let's go talk to him."

They approached Joel Morrison, and Dee Dee tapped him on the shoulder. When he turned to her, she said, "Linda and I need a minute of your time."

"Sure, Sweetie. What's up?"

"Not here, Dad." Dee Dee glanced around the ballroom full of wedding guests eating and dancing. "We need to go some place private."

"All right." Joel turned and led them out of the ballroom and down the hall to his prayer room. "Come in here," he said, holding the door for them.

They walked in, and Joel directed them to the bench Linda knew he usually sat on while he prayed. He pulled up a chair and sat across from them, saying nothing, just waiting.

"The thing is…" Linda began.

And on and on the conversation went, until Linda, with Dee Dee's help, had confessed all her sins. Shame filled her heart with each exposed transgression. Tears filled her eyes and rolled down her cheeks. But Linda noticed that Joel showed no signs of condemnation toward her. Relaxing a bit, she laid it all on the line. "I need your help."

He put his hand over hers. "How can I help you, Daughter?"

At those words, Linda cried some more. That Joel could still think of her as his daughter, after all she had done to his son, was like music to her ears. "Eric is worried that if we pay for Terrell's rehabilitation, people will somehow know that I was the one who hit his car. So, I would like you to make an anonymous donation to the rehab facility where Terrell needs to go. If you can do that for me, I'll get a job and pay you back every penny, I swear."

Joel waved a hand dismissively in the air. "I'll take care of the rehab, and you don't need to worry about paying back a thing. But I do want you to do something for me."

"Anything, just name it," Linda said.

"Let me pray for you."

Linda was dumbfounded. "I'm asking for two hundred and fifty thousand dollars, and all you want from me is that I allow you to pray for me?"

Dee Dee put her hand on Linda's arm. "It's a pretty good offer. Dad prayed for me the last time Drake and I visited, and I haven't been the same since."

Linda turned back to Joel. "Yes, please pray for me."

The three of them held hands, and Joel began, "Heavenly Father, I come boldly to Your throne of grace tonight, lifting You up and giving You all the glory, for You, and You only, are worthy of all my praise. But tonight, Father, I need to let You know that my daughter's heart is heavy with guilt and shame for the things she has done. But You, heavenly Father, have the power to lift her head and give her a reason to smile. Release her from the hold alcohol has over her, and restore her family. Save every member of her household and allow each of them to serve You as never before...."

Joel went on praying like that for about ten minutes. When he was done, Linda and Dee Dee wiped their weeping eyes, and Linda told her father-in-law, "I do want to stop drinking. I just don't know how. Every time I go a day without a drink, I get the shakes."

He hugged her, as did Dee Dee.

"You might need to check yourself into a clinic," Joel said, "so that your withdrawal symptoms can be monitored and dealt with around the clock. Are you willing to do that?"

Linda nodded. "I'm willing to do just about anything right now to turn my life around and save my family."

He patted her on the shoulder as he stood up. "Come on. Let's go find Eric and let him in on this wonderful news."

Six

The news was not so wonderful to Eric. "Not gonna happen. Not as long as she's still married to me." He stood in the prayer room with his father and Linda, but prayer seemed to be the last thing on his mind. "If Linda checks into a clinic for treatment for her alcoholism, I'm finished. I can kiss this next election good-bye."

"But, Son, your first duty is to your wife—don't you know that?" his father pleaded.

Eric glanced at Linda, then turned back to his father. "Linda hasn't been a wife to me in a long time," he spat. "And now you expect me to just throw away my future to help her? I kept her out of jail after she hit that football player, and that's all I'm willing to do."

Linda put her hand on his shoulder, but he recoiled. Just days ago, a rebuke like that would have killed her inside, but not now. Eric was right. She had not been a good wife or mother for many years. But her father-in-law's prayer had given her the strength she needed to decide to make a change.

"I'm sorry that I haven't been the wife you wanted," she told Eric. "I want to be that for you, but I can't do this on my own...I need help."

"Why are you so weak?" he asked, with venom in his voice.

She had no defense; she just stood there with her head down. No one was going to throw a parade for the town drunk; she would have to get sober and throw her own parade. *Yeah, that's it,* she thought. *I'll get sober and then take Kivonna to as many parades as I can find.*

"Listen to me, Son," Joel began. "I know that going through the process of helping Linda to get well won't be good for your campaign, but we've got to help her."

Eric shoved his hands in his pockets.

"What if she had a live-in nurse at home," Joel suggested, "to help her through the withdrawal process?"

"She is not bringing this into our home," Eric barked. "All I would need is for a reporter to get wind of it."

"Then she'll stay here with me," Joel said, with finality in his voice. "I'll hire a nurse to help her kick the habit."

"Fine, do what you want. Kivonna and I are leaving in the morning." Eric stomped out of the room without so much as a backward glance at Linda, the woman he had promised to love, honor, and cherish forever.

Joel took Linda in his arms and rubbed her back as she cried. "It's going to get better, sweetheart. Trust God and put this situation in His hands."

"He hates me, Dad," she sobbed.

"I know it seems like that right now," he whispered, "but I've got a feeling that there is enough love in you to change a man's heart and mind."

∽

"Daddy, why are we leaving Mommy?" Kivonna asked Eric as they rode in the limo to the airport.

"Mommy's not feeling well, so she's going to stay with Grandpa Joel for a while."

"But you always take care of Mommy when she's sick. And she's always sick. Why is that anyway?" Kivonna asked, with anger in her tone.

Eric turned his head and looked out the window. Each block they passed was like the passage of time. In his mind's eye, he pictured Linda dancing, and tears sprang to his eyes. Linda had loved to dance, and he had loved watching her. There had been a time when he had loved every little thing about his wife—her laughter; the way she smiled at him. For Eric, her very presence had been able to light up a room.

But then, after the miscarriages, she'd started drinking, and Eric couldn't remember how many times he'd told Kivonna that she couldn't see her mom because she was sick. Or that her mom couldn't take her to school because she was sick.

"Daddy, don't be sad." Kivonna tugged on his shirt, bringing him back to the present. "When I grow up, I'm going to take over your job as mayor so you can look after Mommy."

It did Eric's heart good to know that his child wanted to follow in his footsteps. But he didn't know if he could continue "looking after" Linda.

True to her word, Linda stayed with Joel and began the process of detoxification. Her mind was set on doing the right thing. She endured the shakes, but by the third day—when sweat poured from her face like a waterfall, she started feeling nauseous, and her eye developed a twitch—she was ready to scream uncle and throw in the towel.

Linda tried to pull herself out of bed, but her nurse—a drill sergeant by the name of Betty Farley, dressed in light blue scrubs with a butterfly print—stopped her. "Stay right there. I'm about to bring you something to eat."

"I can't eat anything. I'm about to throw up."

"You won't throw up. Now, lie down and let me go get your soup."

"What if I have the flu? Maybe I need some NyQuil."

Nurse Betty threw her head back and laughed.

"What's so funny?" Linda demanded. She felt miserable and wanted to be anywhere but here.

"I've been doing this for years, and just about every patient I get tries to pull the ol' NyQuil trick on me. But I've got news for you, Mrs. Linda: Every medicine cabinet in this house has been scrubbed clean of any and all medications that might be able to give you that buzz you want right now."

Linda turned away from the woman. "How can you be so cruel? I'm sweaty and nauseous." She put her hand to her face, trying to stop her eye from its uncontrollable movements. "My eye is twitching. Can't you see that I'm hurting?"

Nurse Betty's voice held a bit more compassion as she said, "You're in withdrawal, hon. It hurts now, but you'll be stronger once it's over."

"I don't want to be stronger. I want a drink." She turned to Betty and pleaded, "Can't you get me just a little something? Just enough to take away the nausea?"

The bedroom door opened, and Joel walked in. "You don't want that, Daughter."

Linda closed her eyes. "I'm sorry I'm such a disappointment, Dad, but I do. I swear, I need a drink."

"No, what you need is to win your family back, and liquor won't help you do that." He sat down in the chair next to her bed. In his hand was his big, well-worn Bible.

"Has Eric called?" Linda asked, just as she did every day.

"Not yet, sweetheart, but you've got to give him time. And remember, it takes two to give up." He opened his Bible. "I want to read you a passage from a book that brings me comfort. Is that okay with you?"

In all the years she had been married to her husband, why had she never noticed what a kind, loving man Eric's father was? She had always believed that Joel played favorites—that he preferred Isaiah and Elaine, just because they served God like he did. As a result, she had been busy fighting against an injustice that had never been there, trying to make sure that Eric didn't get the short end of the stick. Now that she had been given an opportunity to get to know this man, however, she realized that he didn't play favorites. He loved all of his children unconditionally, and that was it. End of story. "Yes, Dad, please read something to me. Maybe it will take my mind off of how miserable I feel right now."

He nodded. "This is from the book of Matthew, chapter seven, beginning with verse seven.

> *Ask, and it shall be given you; seek, and ye shall find; knock, and it shall be opened unto you: for every one that asketh receiveth; and he that seeketh findeth; and to him that knocketh it shall be opened. Or what man is there of you, whom if his son ask bread, will he give him a stone? Or if he ask a fish, will he give him a serpent? If ye then, being evil, know how to give good gifts unto your children, how much more shall your Father which is in heaven give good things to them that ask him? Therefore all things whatsoever ye would that men should do to you, do ye even so to them: for this is the law and the prophets.*

Joel closed his Bible and turned to Linda. "Tell God what you need, sweetheart. He can handle your business better than you ever could."

⌐⌐⌐

Eric was in his office with Darien, discussing their strategy to win the governorship. The problem was, his election prospects had just taken a nasty detour that he would have to battle his way out of. The much-beloved mayor from another city in Ohio had just thrown his hat into the race.

He slumped in his chair. "With Tom Johnson running, we'll have to fight through a primary before I can take it to the governorship."

"Don't worry, buddy. You'll get that nomination, if it's the last thing I do on earth."

"All right, now, don't dig yourself an early grave."

Darien laughed. "But seriously, man, we need to define ourselves in the campaign, and we need to do it soon."

"I hear you."

"I've been thinking," Darien began, "you still haven't done anything with that foundation you're supposed to set up for your father, have you?"

"No, I've been too busy with work. My brother hired someone to help him get his foundation up and running...and then he ended up married to her."

"Isaiah might think of that as a plus."

"Yeah, I'm sure he does," Eric said, remembering how happy Isaiah seemed as he'd made his marriage vows to Ramona this past weekend.

Darien stood. "I need to get going, but you've got to think about using that money to do some good in this state. Like helping people with their mortgages, loaning money so they can start a business... things that will get your name and face out there as someone who cares about the people." He headed for the door, then turned back to Eric. "Colleen Mills will be filling in for me while I'm gone, so you can start working out some of the details with her. You two will be working *very* closely together for the next few weeks."

"I don't like the way that sounds," Eric said.

"Oh, let's just say that I have it on very good authority that Colleen has the hots for a certain mayor who'll soon be the governor of Ohio."

"I won't be the governor of anything if I start up an affair with some woman."

"Colleen is discreet. You won't have to worry about anything getting out."

Eric stood up and walked over to his friend. "How long have you known me, Darien?"

"Since college. Why?"

"Have you ever known me to cheat on Linda?"

Darien shook his head. "No, man, you never have. Look, I know you have this whole honor code that you live by. But you're not happy, and I just want to help you get your happy back, that's all." Darien reached in his pocket and handed Eric a business card. "Here, take this."

"What's this about?"

"I'm tired of seeing you moping around here. If you want a divorce, I found someone who can handle it discreet and quiet-like."

Eric looked at the card, trying to decide what he really wanted. His father's life had been a testament to how wonderful the union of marriage could be. The poor man must cry to his God every night about his disappointment with his children and their marriage woes. Eric lowered his head. "Thanks. I'll give him a call."

Darien put his hand on Eric's shoulder. "I'll see you later. I have a few meetings scheduled this afternoon with your fund-raising committee."

"Do I need to be there?"

"Naw, man. You just stay here and take care of your business. Maybe the next time I see you, you'll even have a smile on your face."

"I'm sure I'll see you tomorrow, but I don't think I'll be smiling by then."

"Get your mind back in the game, bro. I just told you that I'm leaving. I'm outta here for about three weeks—one for vacation, the other two for setting up offices in at least seven different cities. We've got to get the jump on the competition."

Eric eyed his friend. "Send someone else to replace you, Darien. I don't want to see Colleen in my office." He walked back to his desk and found himself staring at the business card of the man who could take him out of his misery.

The phone on his desk rang, and Eric jumped. He put the card down and answered the phone. "Mayor Morrison speaking."

"Hey, Son! It's good to hear your voice."

Eric knew his father had meant the comment as a criticism, since he hadn't called to check on Linda in the four days that she'd been away from home. "How are you, Dad?"

"I'm doing good. It's your wife I'm worried about."

"Why is that?"

"She has a fever today. She's trying real hard to kick this thing, Son, but she needs you right now."

"I've been busy, Dad."

"Can you at least call her? She asks me every day if you've called. She's trying to be strong, but I can tell that it breaks her heart every time I have to admit that you haven't called."

"I'll call her tonight. Right now, I need to get back to work, okay?"

"All right, Son. You take care of your business there. But don't forget about your business here."

After hanging up, Eric sat down in his chair and stared at the business card again. He could divorce Linda and be free from all her drama...free from all the lies. He just prayed that she would go quietly and not put up a fuss. After all, she owed him big time. If it weren't for the lie he'd told to cover her tracks, she would be in prison for driving under the influence. Ironically, it was the lie he'd told that made it impossible for him to look his wife in the face anymore. He'd lost his integrity because of her, and now he just wanted out.

Seven

Day five, and I'm still alive! Linda kept chanting to herself. The call from Eric and Kivonna the night before had helped, giving her strength to make it through the night. Now that her fever had broken, she dared to believe that she could actually become clean and sober again.

She had a lot of work to do to rebuild her family, but somehow she would find a way to turn things around with Eric and Kivonna. She felt nothing but shame for the way she'd allowed her weakness to take over her life for the past five years. Her daughter was nine now, halfway to eighteen. Linda doubted that Kivonna could remember her early years, when her mom had been sober. Tears flowed down her face, and she had to stop herself from dwelling on how much she might have damaged her child; if she kept thinking about it, she would get up from her bed and go find herself a drink to numb the pain. And that was the last thing she wanted to do.

There was a knock on her door. Linda was grateful for the interruption. "Come in," she said, wiping the tears from her face.

Joel walked in with his trusty Bible, and Linda found herself smiling, wondering what he would read to her today.

"Good morning, Daughter. Nurse Betty told me that your fever is gone."

She nodded. "I think I'm going to make it, Dad."

"What's this 'I think' business? I *know* that you're going to make it."

She gave him a half smile, then looked at the Bible in his hand. "So, what are you going to read to me today?"

Joel set the Bible on the nightstand. "God directed me to some Scriptures that you need to meditate on, but before I read them to you, I come bringing good news."

"What?" Now she gave him a big grin. She hadn't heard any good news in a long while and was anxious to know what her father-in-law had to tell her.

He clasped his hands together. "Terrell Anderson left the hospital today and was transported to a top-notch sports rehabilitation clinic, where he'll receive the best possible care. You don't have to worry about him anymore."

Never in all her life had she felt so much joy over a blessing that belonged to someone else. Her heart was so overwhelmed that she covered her face with her hands, trying desperately not to cry. "Thank you for doing that for me. Thank you so much!"

"It was my pleasure," Joel said. When she looked at him again, he was sitting down and had picked up his Bible. "Now, young lady, during my prayer time this morning, the Lord showed me that you've been guilt-tripping yourself over some of the things you've done in the past."

"My very recent past," she reminded him.

"It doesn't matter. The past is the past. Once God cleans you up, no man can ever call you unclean again."

Linda turned her head away, unable to face her father-in-law. He was a good man, and she was scared—of her past and her future.

"I'm going to read you Psalm Fifty-one, so you can see that you aren't the only one who's ever felt like she did so much wrong that there is nowhere to turn." He flipped a few pages and began reading:

Have mercy upon me, O God, according to thy lovingkindness: according unto the multitude of thy tender mercies blot out my transgressions. Wash me thoroughly from mine iniquity, and cleanse me from my sin. For I acknowledge my transgressions: and my sin is ever before me. Against thee, thee only, have I sinned, and done this evil in thy sight: that thou mightest be justified when thou speakest, and be clear when thou judgest. Behold, I was shapen in iniquity, and in sin did my mother conceive me. Behold, thou desirest truth in the inward parts: and in the hidden part thou shalt make me to know wisdom. Purge me with hyssop, and I shall be clean: wash me, and I shall be whiter than snow. Make me to hear joy and gladness; that the bones which thou hast broken may rejoice. Hide thy face from my sins, and blot out all mine iniquities. Create in me a clean heart, O God; and renew a right spirit within me. Cast me not away from thy presence; and take not thy holy spirit from me. Restore unto me the joy of thy salvation; and uphold me with thy free spirit. Then will I teach transgressors thy ways; and sinners shall be converted unto thee. Deliver me from bloodguiltiness, O God, thou God of my salvation: and my tongue shall sing aloud of thy righteousness. O Lord, open thou my lips; and my mouth shall show forth thy praise. For thou desirest not sacrifice; else would I give it: thou delightest not in burnt offering. The sacrifices of God are a broken spirit: a broken and a contrite heart, O God, thou wilt not despise. Do good in thy good pleasure unto Zion: build thou the walls of Jerusalem. Then shalt thou be pleased with the sacrifices of righteousness, with burnt offering and whole burnt offering: then shall they offer bullocks upon thine altar.

When he closed the Book, he looked up at Linda. Tears were flowing down her face.

"That's exactly how I feel," she whispered, "except it seems as if I've sinned against God, Eric, and Kivonna. I don't know how to fix that."

"Remember what the Good Book said—the only sacrifice God requires is that of a broken spirit and a contrite heart. Turn to Him, Linda. God will cleanse and heal you, and then He will help you get your family back." Joel stood and turned to leave.

Linda touched his hand, stopping him. When he turned back to face her, she said, "Thank you."

"Sure, sweetheart. Now, try to get some sleep. You'll be ready to go back home soon. You'll need to be rested up for that." Joel left the room, humming a song that Linda didn't recognize, but she instinctively knew it was a song of praise to God.

Joel had told her to get some sleep, but Linda was too busy wondering whether she would ever be able to sing a song of praise to God. Wondering if her family members would ever trust her with their hearts again. When she was done wondering, she turned her thoughts to the three miscarriages she'd had, which had turned her world upside down.

Each miscarriage had sent her further and further into a black hole of depression, until she'd found herself unable to deal with life and all of its miserable realities. Eric had never understood why she couldn't be strong like him and just be happy with the one child they did have. But Eric had a job to go off to every morning. People who needed him. Decisions that had to be made. She had nothing to take her mind off of her three forgotten-by-everybody-but-her children.

Just as she was about to dive back into the abyss of despair, she remembered the Scripture passage that Joel had read to her the other day—the one about her ability to ask God for what she needed and trust that He would provide it. She turned her face toward heaven and stepped up to God like she had every right to come before His throne of grace.

"What can I say, Lord? I see now that You have tried to be good to me. I had a family that loved me, but, these days, it seems as if the love is gone. I don't blame them; I'm the one who messed up. But with Your help, I believe I can get back everything that Joel said the devil has tried to steal from me.

"I want to give my life to You. All I ask is that You help me stay away from alcohol. If You can do that, I believe that life can be beautiful again. I now understand that my husband and daughter are precious, and I want to go home and show them how much they mean to me. In Jesus' name, amen."

~

"So, how discreet can you be?" Eric asked his lawyer, Thomas Hopkins, as they sat in the attorney's office.

"I'm going to be real honest with you, Mayor Morrison: You are a political figure, and if your wife is the ticking time bomb that Darien described, I can't guarantee that we can keep this quiet."

Why did Darien describe Linda in such a derogatory manner to this man? Eric wanted to know. Even though he was the one who wanted the divorce, he didn't feel comfortable bad-mouthing his wife. "I don't know what Darien told you, but, although Linda and I have our differences, she's not some evil, despicable person."

"Then why do you want a divorce?"

Eric averted his eyes. "She's done some things that I just can't forgive. I don't see how I can stay married to her while I'm feeling like this."

"And yet, you don't want word of this divorce to get out before next year's election?"

"Is that possible?" Eric asked, his voice hopeful.

Thomas leaned forward and rubbed his hands together. "I think you have a better chance of seeing this blow up in your face on CNN than divorcing your wife in secret—especially if she doesn't want the divorce."

That gave Eric an idea. "What if she's the one who files for divorce?"

Thomas smiled at that. "We could always spin it to make you look like the aggrieved party. You tried everything to make your marriage work, but your wife is walking around with an undiagnosed mental illness...you know, something like that."

Yes, that's what they would do. Linda owed Eric for all of the years he'd stood by her, even as she destroyed his integrity to the point where he didn't even recognize himself anymore. Oh, yeah. She would file for divorce or risk never seeing Kivonna again.

Yet the more he thought on the idea, the more he realized he couldn't threaten Linda with the loss of another child—that would be cruel, and he could never be that cruel to her. He would just have to find another way to get her to file those papers.

Eight

When Linda got home, the house was empty. She went to the refrigerator and grabbed a green apple and a bottle of water. She'd lost ten pounds at her father-in-law's, detoxing from the "demon liquor," as Joel had called it. On the plane ride, Linda had set herself a goal of dropping another ten pounds, to get back down to her ideal weight of 140. She didn't believe she had to be a stick figure to be beautiful. She saw nothing attractive about having her bones and rib cage practically poking through her skin. She had looked good at 140 pounds; it had been those extra twenty pounds she'd put on that had caused her face to swell and stomach to protrude. So, first thing tomorrow, she was going back to the gym.

She headed upstairs, tossing and catching her apple like a baseball. Halfway up, she noticed that she was humming. She stopped and smiled. Had her father-in-law really rubbed off on her that much? Linda could only hope so.

In her bedroom, she picked up the phone and called Dee Dee. That was another thing that had changed. She and Dee Dee had never gotten along. Linda had always found Dee Dee self-important, pretentious, and just downright mean. And Dee Dee had been all those things, but then, as Dee Dee had told her, she'd given her life to the Lord. Now that Linda had done the same, she and Dee Dee had something in common.

When Dee Dee answered the phone, Linda said, "I just called to thank you for everything you've done for me."

"No thanks needed, girl. What are sisters for?"

"Dee Dee, you don't understand. If you hadn't gone out of your way to help me last week, I don't know if I ever would have had the courage to stop drinking or to give my life to God. But I did both of those things." Her voice caught as tears came to her eyes. "And I have you to thank for it."

"Oh, Linda, I'm so glad to hear that everything worked out for you. Drake and I have been praying for you all week long. Daddy said you were doing well, but he never said anything about you inviting the Lord into your heart."

Linda wiped the tears from her face. "It happened just two nights ago. God has taken the taste for alcohol out of my mouth, and I will be His disciple for the rest of my life. I want to run out into the streets and proclaim to the world how He freed me from bondage to alcohol."

"What did Eric say when you told him?"

The smile on Linda's face evaporated. "I haven't talked to him since it happened. I'm home now, but no one is here."

There was silence on the line, and then Dee Dee said, "If you don't mind, I'd like to give you a bit of advice."

"I could use some advice." Linda sighed. "To tell you the truth, I don't think Eric really wanted me to come back home."

"Oh, Linda, don't say that," Dee Dee told her. "But don't try to push him, or make him believe that you've changed. Just show him day by day, with your actions. I thank God that Drake didn't give up on me. Don't you let Eric get away with giving up on you."

"Okay," Linda said, then decided to change the subject. "Guess what?"

"What?"

"I lost ten pounds! I'm going back to the gym, starting tomorrow, so that I can lose some more."

"That's great, Linda!" Dee Dee paused. "And I owe you an apology. Through the years, I've said a lot of mean things to you. But I should have never called you fat. You are not fat, and I hope you don't feel the need to lose weight because of anything I said."

"You are forgiven, Dee Dee. And don't worry; I'm not talking about anything drastic. I just want to take off another ten pounds."

"Go for it, girl! I'm all for lightening the load."

Linda laughed. "Let me get off this phone and get myself prepared to get my family back."

"All right. I'll talk to you later, Sis."

Linda smiled as she hung up the phone, liking the idea of Dee Dee and her being sisters. She went into the bathroom and ran a bubble bath. She turned her radio to the "oldies but goodies" station, then immersed her body in the hot water. The sensation felt wonderful. In the early years of her marriage, Linda had loved to soak in the tub while reading romance novels or listening to music. Eric would come in and soap her back for her. Then she'd try her best to get rid of him so that she could continue with her "me" time. Of course, she would usually lose that battle, and Eric would join her in the tub, grinning and saying, "Why do you think I ordered the larger tub with the whirlpool jets?"

"Because you know that I love to soak in the tub," she would answer.

"Because I planned to ambush you in here," he'd counter. "Move over, woman; I need you to soap my back now."

She would laugh and then oblige him.

All that had ended the time she'd added a bottle of wine to her favorite ritual. She'd ended up drinking so much that she'd fallen asleep in the tub. If Eric hadn't come into the bathroom and found her when he had, she probably would have drowned. At that point, he'd made her promise to take only showers—no more baths. Thus, another consequence of her drinking had been the loss of her "me" time.

It felt so good to be able to resume the ritual. Linda turned on the jets and closed her eyes. She leaned back against the wall of the tub and let the music take her back down memory lane.

Linda didn't know how much time had passed when the bathroom door opened and Eric burst in.

"Linda!" he barked. "I thought we agreed that you wouldn't take baths anymore."

"Calm down, Eric. I'm okay. I'm not drinking, so there's no reason why I can't soak in the tub."

"You were asleep."

"No, I just had my eyes closed. I was enjoying the music, like I used to do." Teddy Pendergrass's "Feel the Fire" was playing. She wanted to reach out and touch her husband, but she had lost his love.

She saw the pain in his eyes as he turned away from her.

"Eric, I'm better now. I really am."

He walked out of the bathroom without another word.

Give him time, Linda, give him time, she reminded herself. She needed to be patient. Eric had suffered through years of her alcohol abuse, and there was no way that he was going to trust that she was done with all of that just because she said so.

She unplugged the stopper and got out of the tub. After drying herself off and putting on some loungewear, she went in search of Kivonna.

She found her daughter in the kitchen, chatting away with Eric. That is, until she walked in. Kivonna's mouth clamped shut, and she sat there, staring at Linda, looking unsure of what to do.

Linda walked over to her daughter and wrapped her arms around her. "I missed you so much, Honey. I'm so glad to be home with you and your father."

Kivonna had stiffened at her touch, and her arms hung limply at her sides.

Linda stepped back, trying her best not to cry. "How have you been doing?"

"I'm okay," Kivonna said.

"I was hoping that you and I could spend some time together this weekend. Would you like to go to the mall with your mom?"

Kivonna's eyes shifted to Eric and then back to her. "Daddy says I can't ride with you."

Linda was offended. She wanted to lash out at Eric for saying that to their daughter, but she knew that wouldn't win her any points with Kivonna. So, she simply said, "I don't have a car right now, anyway. How about we catch a cab to the mall? We can do a little shopping...maybe see a movie. Then maybe your dad would pick us up."

Kivonna's eyes brightened, and she turned to Eric. "Would you, Daddy?"

"Sure thing, sweetheart. Just let me know when and where."

Turning back to Linda, Kivonna said, "Daddy bought me the new *Lion King* DVD. Do you want to watch it with me tonight?"

"I'd love to. Just let me grab a sandwich and I'm all yours." Linda opened the refrigerator and then asked, "Do you want a sandwich also?"

"Naw, Daddy and I just ate some pizza."

Linda and Kivonna went into the family room, kicked their feet up, and watched the movie together. It was the first mother/daughter movie night they had shared in a long time. Kivonna ended up falling asleep with her head in Linda's lap, so Linda carried her upstairs and put her to bed.

When she walked into her bedroom, Eric was sitting in one of the lounge chairs, watching the local news. On the screen flashed some photos of Terrell Anderson at his rehabilitation facility. Eric turned the television off and glared at her. "I guess you got what you wanted."

She willed herself to not be intimidated. "It was the right thing to do, Eric. Your father donated that money anonymously, so no one will ever know where it came from."

"That's what you think. But trust me when I say that word will get out."

She walked over and sat down in the chair next to him. "What's wrong, Eric? This isn't like you. The man I married was always willing to lend a helping hand."

"You've changed me, Linda—or haven't you noticed what a liar I've become?"

And that was the crux of their problem. The moment Eric had told his first lie to protect her, their relationship had been doomed. He was a man who prided himself on integrity; that had been what she loved most about him when they'd first gotten together. Eric had wanted to be king of the world, and he'd told her that he would never lie, cheat, or steal in order to accomplish his goals. But here they were, and it was her fault.

"All I can say is that I'm sorry," Linda said, "and that I'm fighting hard to make sure nothing like that ever happens again."

"A little late for all that, isn't it?"

She shook her head. "I don't think so, and neither does your father."

Eric rolled his eyes. "My father is a sucker for a hard-luck story. The man takes in stray cats, so don't think that what he did for you was anything special."

She touched Eric's leg; he scooted away. Ignoring the slight, she said, "I will always consider what your father did for me as something special. With his help, I've changed my life."

Eric wasn't buying it. "Look, Linda. You might as well know that I don't intend to sleep in this room with you. I was waiting in here because I wanted to talk to you about something."

"Okay," she said slowly. "Shoot."

"First, I want to make sure that you're doing okay...I mean, you're on firm footing, right?"

"Yes, Eric, I've never felt better."

"Good." He hesitated for a moment, then said, "I want a divorce."

As if she'd been slapped, Linda reared her head back. "Excuse me?"

"You heard me. I want a divorce, but I need your help."

Drawing out each word, she said, "Let me get this straight: You want me to help you divorce...me?"

Eric nodded. "After all I've done for you over the years, I figure it's the least you can do for me. The bottom line is, it would hurt my campaign if I initiated the divorce proceedings. So, I want you to do it."

Her body shook from the fear that his words brought to her very being. She couldn't live without Eric—simply refused to. Standing up, she angrily pointed a finger at him. "Now, you listen to me, Eric Morrison. I have loved you for so long that I don't know how to stop. Maybe you can simply dismiss me, but I'll never do such a thing to you. So, either divorce me yourself, or give me a chance to prove to you that I've changed. Because I will never divorce you—do you hear me? Never!"

He opened his mouth to respond, but Linda lifted a hand to silence him.

"I don't want to talk to you anymore tonight," she told him. "Please leave my room."

Eric stood but made no move to leave.

Linda walked over to the nightstand, opened the bottom drawer, and pulled out the Bible that Eric's father had given them on their wedding day. Neither of them had ever bothered to read it, but they'd kept it because it had come from Joel. Now, Linda felt compelled to read every word in the Book. She needed to receive counsel from God on how to handle a husband who didn't want to be a husband anymore. She needed a diversion to keep from doing what she wanted to do at that moment: knock some sense into Eric.

She got into bed, opened her Bible, and then looked over at Eric, who stood by the door, staring at her. His face showed total confusion—and she couldn't blame him. He probably didn't recognize her. The Linda of recent years would have been on her knees, begging him not to leave her, not ordering him out of her room. With any luck, he'd realize, as she just had, that she was acting more like the Linda he'd married over a decade ago.

Nine

Linda had been home for two weeks, and the house was still a liquor-free zone. She and Eric were not exactly on the best of terms, because he refused to believe that she was serious about having made a change. She ignored his attitude, taking care of the house and making sure that dinner was ready when he arrived home every night. The only thing that she asked of him was that he eat with the family. He granted her request, but it was like pulling teeth to get him to join in on the conversation.

One morning, he had the audacity to ask her to plan a dinner party for him. After she agreed, he pointed a finger at her and said, "No booze." As if she was just itching for a reason to bring alcohol back into their home.

She didn't respond to his insult but turned away from him, picked up her gym bag, and left the house. She had a new Lexus, and she was determined to take better care of this one than she had the last.

At the gym, under the direction of her personal trainer, Linda wore herself out running on the treadmill and doing twenty minutes on the elliptical machine. Next, she lifted weights for fifteen minutes, followed by a Zumba class. Halfway through Zumba, Linda wondered at the sanity of joining this weight-loss boot camp. The good news was, she had lost another five pounds and was now able to wear the clothes she'd pushed to the back of her closet about three years ago.

When she was done with her workout, she showered and changed. As she headed to her car, a woman called her name. Linda turned around and saw Susan Humphrey coming toward her. Linda smiled. "Hey, Susan! How've you been?"

"Not too good, to tell you the truth."

Linda was surprised at the woman's candor. She'd known Susan for a few years. Her children attended school with Kivonna, and Susan's husband was a member of the city council, so they often saw each other at various political functions. But they had never really been close personal friends. "I'm sorry to hear that," Linda said.

"Look, I'm not going to beat around the bush," Susan said. "How did you kick the booze?"

"What?" There was no way Linda had heard this woman correctly.

Susan held up a hand. "I'm not trying to get in your business or anything." She sighed. "You see, I've been drinking for a long time. I thought I could handle it, but it's finally taking a toll on my marriage, and...well, Harry left me."

Linda felt naked and exposed, standing in the parking lot with a woman to whom she'd never confided a single thing. "How did you know?" was all she could say.

"Oh, don't worry; I'm not sure if others in our circle noticed, but you and I have the same problem...or *had* the same problem. So, I noticed, and I could also tell that you had kicked the habit."

"You're right," Linda whispered, as if a gang of reporters would rush over at any moment and demand that she admit to having hit Terrell Anderson while driving drunk.

"Can you help me?" Susan asked.

"All I can do is tell you what worked for me. Are you interested?" Susan nodded.

"Great. Would you like to grab lunch or something?"

"I would love to."

Over lunch, Linda told the woman how her father-in-law had prayed with her and read the Bible to her while she had suffered through alcohol withdrawal. But Linda didn't want to make the situation sound like it had been a walk through the park; like a little prayer and Bible reading, and—presto—she was cured. "Abstaining from alcohol is the hardest thing I've ever had to do in my life," she confessed.

"But you did it," Susan reminded her.

"It's been only a few weeks. I have to guard against drinking every day. But I think I know of a way that we can help each other."

"That sounds good." Susan nodded. "I'm game for whatever you want to do."

A few days later, Linda was in the kitchen with Maria, going over the dinner menu for Eric's grand affair, which was scheduled to take place the following Thursday evening. She had sent out special invitations to the individuals on Eric's guest list. Each of them had been a high-dollar donor to his campaign for mayor, and Eric was hoping to win their support for his gubernatorial run. And Linda intended to make it an evening they wouldn't soon forget.

"I am not a fan of asparagus," Linda said, "but I love the way you fix it, so include that on the menu."

"Yes, ma'am." Maria marked her list. "For the appetizer, I was thinking I'd make that potato soup Mr. Morrison likes. Will that be okay?"

"Your potato soup is wonderful." Linda nodded. "What about the meat?"

"We could do Cornish hens…or what about steak and lobster?"

"I think I'd like the Cornish hens with garlic mashed potatoes and asparagus."

"If we're going to do the garlic mashed potatoes, maybe I should fix a cauliflower or broccoli soup?"

"Either one is fine with me. I haven't tasted a soup of yours that I didn't want to get seconds and even thirds of."

Maria laughed. The phone rang, and she went to answer it. "Morrison residence. How may I help you?" There was a pause, and then Maria said, "May I tell her who's calling?"

"Who is it?" Linda asked, anxious to get back to the menu planning.

"Terrell Anderson, ma'am. He wants to speak to you."

The shock registered on her face before she had time to mask it. She stood up from the counter and started for the hall. "I'll take it upstairs," she said, over her shoulder. "Would you please prepare three of your best desserts, so I can have Eric sample them and make a decision?"

"I'll get it done right away."

"Thanks, Maria. And for dinner tonight, I'd like some of your fabulous lasagna and garlic bread."

"I thought you were on a diet!" Maria teased.

Linda smiled. "I've been eating right for days; a little splurge now and then won't hurt."

Once she had reached her bedroom, she took a deep breath, picked up the phone, and asked Maria to hang up. "Hello, this is Linda Morrison."

"Mrs. Morrison, it's Terrell Anderson. I just wanted to call and give an update on my progress, so you can quit trying to pump the nurses for information."

"Excuse me? I don't think I know what you're talking about."

"Mrs. Morrison, this facility has caller ID. They know that someone from your house has been calling every day, asking questions."

She opened her mouth to protest her innocence, but she'd read in her Bible that very morning something about a liar not being able to tarry in God's sight, and the memory stopped her cold. "I was concerned about you. I just wanted to make sure your leg was healing."

"And I called to answer your questions, but first, I need you to answer a few questions for me."

She swallowed her anxiety. "Ask away."

"I keep having these mental flashbacks of the crash. They've been giving me a headache because I don't understand them. So, this may sound crazy, but are you sure it wasn't you driving the car that hit me? I know the police said it was your gardener, but...."

Linda went completely still. Eric was going to stop waiting for her to divorce him—this information would propel him to just go ahead and divorce her himself. But, wait! This was her moment—her chance to be free from the guilt she had locked away. She closed her eyes. "You're right...it was me," she confessed.

When the line went silent, Linda rushed on. "Terrell, I need you to understand that I was unconscious after I hit you. I didn't run from the scene of the crime. Some people who wanted to help me pulled me out of the car and drove me home."

"That's it!" Terrell shouted. "That's the dream I keep having."

"Are you okay, Terrell?"

He lowered his voice. "I didn't understand it, but I kept seeing this man pulling a woman out of a car and placing her in another car. When that car drove off, a man ran over to me and told me not to worry, because he was calling an ambulance. I was going in and out of consciousness myself, so I couldn't even remember the man's face."

"That was Michael, my gardener. He didn't mean any harm, Terrell. He was just trying to help. His son pulled me out of the car, and then Michael took my place at the crash site."

"Had you been drinking or something?" Terrell asked, his tone accusatory.

Shame filled her very being; she wanted to run from the truth, but it was ever before her. She felt a strength coming from somewhere, and she knew it had to be God helping her walk through the fire. "Yes, Terrell, I had been drinking that night."

"Are you crazy, lady? You could have killed me."

"I know, and I am so sorry. If it helps matters any, I have since stopped drinking, all because of the accident."

"One more question," he said. "Did you pay for my rehab?"

She sighed. So much for anonymity. "I asked my father-in-law to do it. He's a very giving man."

"What about your husband? He wouldn't fork over the money?"

"Look, Terrell. You have every right to be mad at me. I'll take the blame for it all...I'll even go down to the police station and straighten everything out, if you want me to. But my husband had nothing to do with this. It's not his fault that I chose to drive while under the influence."

"You'd really go to the police and tell them the truth about what happened that night?"

She nodded her head, as if he could see her. "The only thing that has stopped me from doing that is knowing how much it would damage my husband's reputation. But you deserve justice for what happened to you, so if that's what you want me to do, I'll do it."

"Look, lady, don't sweat it," he said, to her surprise. "My mom told me that you came to the hospital to check up on me. And I kind of figured you were my anonymous donor. Rehab is going great, by the way. My leg should be a hundred percent better in another month or so."

"Oh, Terrell, I'm happy to hear that!"

There was an awkward silence, and then Terrell said, "Well, just so you know, you can call my room directly the next time you want to check on me."

There was so much she wanted to say at that moment, but "Thank you" was all she could manage.

For the past several weeks, the news had been filled with stories of Terrell's great athletic ability, but that day, Linda had gotten a glimpse at the young man's great compassion. He knew that she was the reason he needed rehab in the first place; and yet, even though he'd been a little angry, his voice had held no vengefulness. He hadn't said it explicitly, but Linda knew that Terrell had forgiven her for what she'd done to him.

She didn't understand what God was doing, but she could see His hand all over the situation. She looked heavenward and prayed, "Lord, thank You for Your grace and for allowing Terrell to forgive me. All I ask is that You would show me how to make this right for Terrell without losing my husband in the process."

She went back downstairs and straightened up the living room, dining room, and family room. When she'd finished, she left the house to pick Kivonna up from school.

Linda parked the car by the curb and smiled as Kivonna ran over. Just a few weeks ago, the child hadn't wanted to be anywhere near a car that her mother was driving. But Linda had regained her daughter's trust. How she wished that her husband was as easy to convince.

"How was school today, Pumpkin?"

Kivonna scrunched up her nose. "Mean ol' Ms. Farley is making us do definitions with our spelling words."

Linda laughed. "I'm sure it won't be that bad. I had to do definitions when I was in grade school, too. But you know what?"

"What?"

"When I took my exams to get into college, knowing those words really paid off."

"All right," Kivonna said, as if she was agreeing to get a tooth pulled. "I'll do it, and then I'll get into a good college, too."

"That's the spirit."

"Mom?"

"Yes, Baby?"

After a bit of hesitation, Kivonna asked, "Are you and Daddy getting a divorce?"

Linda tried to keep her eyes on the road, but the question really alarmed her. "Why would you ask that?"

"Well, my friend Lisa said that after her parents started sleeping in separate rooms, they divorced and then slept in separate houses altogether. Is that going to happen to you and Daddy?"

"I sure hope not." She took her right hand off the steering wheel and squeezed Kivonna's shoulder, trying to comfort her. "Your dad and I love each other very much. But adults don't see eye to eye on everything."

"He's still mad about your drinking, you mean."

She wasn't going to lie to her daughter. She was tired of all of the falsehoods that had been told lately. "That…and some other things. But I believe we will work through these issues. I'm praying every day for our marriage. You can help me pray, if you want to."

Kivonna smiled and leaned back in her seat. "Grandpa always says that prayer is the answer for everything that ails you."

"He's right, Baby."

Once they arrived at home, Linda grabbed a snack from the kitchen for her and Kivonna, then followed the girl into the family room to help her with her homework. When they were finished, Linda left Kivonna to watch some cartoons, while she went and set the table for the evening meal.

When Eric came home, the family gathered for dinner. Linda had observed that, for the last week, Eric had been getting home by six thirty so that they could eat dinner at a reasonable hour. She'd noticed, but she hadn't said anything.

"Lasagna, huh?" Eric said, as Linda set a generous helping in front of him. "One of my favorite dishes Maria makes."

"I know." Linda nodded. "You've been working hard for this city and on your campaign, so I thought you deserved a treat tonight."

He smiled briefly at her, then looked away.

After the meal had been served, Linda sat down. "Who wants to say grace?"

Kivonna raised her hand. "I will! I will!"

Eric and Linda laughed at Kivonna's eagerness. "Go ahead, Baby Girl," Eric said.

Kivonna steepled her hands and prayed, "God bless Mama and Daddy. Help them to like each other again, and bless the food we are about to receive. Amen."

Linda kept her eyes on her plate, too afraid to glance at Eric after the prayer their daughter had just prayed. They ate in silence, until Kivonna finished her meal and asked if she could go play in her room.

As Kivonna left to play by herself, Linda felt a wave of regret. If she had been able to have more children, Kivonna would have a playmate or two. But then, she reminded herself that she had been an only child and had entertained herself for endless hours as a kid. She'd even made up an imaginary friend. Not that she'd gotten away with much mischief, blaming it on poor little Lizzie.

"What are you smiling about?" Eric asked.

"Oh, nothing much. I was just thinking about how I handled being an only child."

"Growing up, there were days that I wished I was an only child."

Linda smiled. "I'm learning to find peace in what I have."

Eric raised his eyebrows. "For years, you've spent more time mourning the children you didn't have than enjoying the one you did. Why the sudden change?"

Linda stood and started collecting the dinner dishes. "It's my new attitude," she told him, with a bit of pep in her step.

"Here, let me help." Eric got to his feet and carried his plate to the kitchen. He scraped off the plates over the garbage bin, while Linda loaded the dishwasher.

With the cleanup finished, they headed for the family room. "So, how was your day?" Linda asked.

"Do you really want to know?"

"Of course. You do a lot for this community; I love hearing about your work."

With his chest puffed out, Eric sat down and told Linda about his day. He also told her about the plan Darien had come up with to increase his name recognition across the state. He told her they planned to use Joel's foundation to help people struggling with mortgages and to provide loans to small businesses.

"Those are good things that will help a great deal of people, Eric."

"I sense a 'but' coming on."

He knew her too well. From the day Linda had begun helping Susan get over her addiction to alcohol, she had been thinking just how many other people she could help, if only Eric would allow her to lead an organization for recovering alcoholics and their families. She would need money to start such an organization, and she'd hoped that Eric would allocate some of his foundation's funds for that purpose. She hadn't had the nerve to ask him yet, but, since he'd already decided on ways to spend the money, Linda figured that she'd better speak up before there was nothing left. "I do want to talk to you about something."

"What's up?"

"Well, I...I was wondering if you'd like to fund an organization that I want to start."

"What kind of organization?"

"I want to help recovering alcoholics—and their families— deal with the issues they will face while in recovery."

"Absolutely not!" he exploded. "What do you think AA is for?"

"AA didn't help me, Eric. It was God and your father. I want to tell the world about the method I found for getting sober."

"I suppose you think everybody has the money to hire a nurse to help with the detox process?"

"No," she said calmly, "but most people have at least one family member or friend willing to stop in and check on them."

"Just when I thought you were finally turning things around...."
He shook his head. "You do that, and—divorce or not—I will
throw you out of this house."

"Alrighty, then." She stood up, straightened her pantsuit, and
looked her husband in the eye. "I love you dearly, Eric, but you've
got one more time to threaten to throw me out of my own home.
Do it again, and I guarantee that you won't like what comes next."
She walked out of the family room, fuming. She needed to read
her Bible like a fish needed to swim. Yet, even as she was headed to
her room to spend some quality time with her Lord, she thought,
*It will be a long time before Eric slaps his lips on another lasagna in
this house.*

Ten

Eric spent a week brooding after Linda had asked him for money to start an organization that would end his political career. Was the woman trying to ruin him on purpose? She knew perfectly well that if she broadcasted to the world that she had been an alcoholic, while he was trying to get his campaign for governor up and running, that would be it for him.

He'd wanted her to react to his moodiness, tell him that she couldn't take it anymore and that she would never again even think about doing such a crazy thing. But Linda just floated around the house, as if she didn't notice how upset he was.

The woman confused him. She bewildered him. But, at the same time, she had ignited a fire within him that he'd thought had died long ago. For about a year now, he'd been her husband in name only. Now he wanted to change that; he just didn't know if he could trust her with his heart again.

"Good evening, Mr. Mayor," said a middle-aged man at the dinner party. He and his wife had more money than they knew what to do with. "Your home is lovely, and the dinner was out of this world."

Eric grinned. "I can't take credit for any of it. My wife keeps the house beautifully, and she and our cook planned the meal, although they did let me pick the dessert."

He received a thumbs-up from the man. "Best red velvet cake I've ever tasted."

"It's the extra cream filling that Maria adds to it," Eric said. "Makes it seem like you're eating cheesecake."

As he turned to speak with another couple who had made a generous donation to his last campaign, a server walked by, holding up a tray of fluted glasses containing what looked like champagne. Eric turned his gaze to Linda. Everything had been going just fine with the dinner party, but now the "fun" would start. Maybe she'd ordered the liquor to humiliate him in front of his guests.

As if reading the question in his eyes, Linda shrugged her shoulders and shook her head.

Eric wasn't buying it. She'd signed off on the entire menu, beverages and all. She was the hostess, for goodness' sake.

Eric was determined to nip it in the bud before things got out of hand. He was headed for the waiter when Darien stopped him. "Hey, man. Linda did a wonderful job. You should really be pleased."

"Yeah, she did," Eric agreed.

"Then I'm trying to figure out why you've got this scowl on your face for all to see."

"She ordered alcohol," Eric hissed. "I specifically told her not to do it, and she did it anyway."

"Is that what's got your knickers in a bunch? Bring it down a notch, man. Linda didn't order the liquor; I did."

"You *what?*"

"You heard me. When I called to inquire about the menu, Maria informed me that Linda was not ordering alcohol for this event. So, I took care of it myself."

Eric closed his eyes and tried to count to ten. He wanted to punch his friend. Linda had been doing her best to make a change. Given how unreasonable he'd been at times, she might have taken a moment to put him in his place, but she'd kept her smile and her dignity. Darien was trying to ruin all of that. When Eric opened his eyes again, his jaw was tight as he asked, "Have you lost your mind? You, of all people, know that my wife is"—he lowered his voice to a whisper—"a recovering alcoholic."

"And you, of all people, should know that the people in this room have money to spend on your campaign. So, if they want liquor, they are going to get it. Heck, I'd even bring in a few strippers if it would get them to write a bigger check."

"So if this sets my wife back, then too bad? Is that how you feel about it?" Eric's fist was clenching as he spoke.

"Hey, you two." Linda walked over and put her hand on Eric's arm. "I don't know what you're arguing about," she said quietly, "but you might want to save it for the office. People are beginning to stare."

Eric looked at his wife, struck by her beauty. He felt like a louse for being so hard on her the past few years. But, as God was his witness, if Linda was able to get through the night without falling back off the wagon, then he would never doubt her again. He leaned down and kissed her on the cheek. "You did a wonderful job with the dinner party, Hon. Thank you."

Clearly surprised by the show of affection, Linda stepped back and smiled at him. "Thank you for the compliment, Mr. Mayor."

Darien took Linda's arm and twirled her around. "Linda, my goodness, what have you been doing with yourself? You look ten years younger."

"Losing twenty pounds will do that for a woman."

"Well, if you ever decide to leave this loser"—he pointed at Eric, who scowled—"you know that I'm still single."

"I know it, and there's a reason for that, Darien," Linda said with a smirk. Then she walked away and began mingling with the guests milling around the living room.

Darien started to say something to Eric, but he ignored him and took off after Linda, trying to catch up with her.

"Hey Linda, wait up," Eric said.

Linda turned around. Another server carrying a tray of fluted glasses passed by, but Linda didn't seem to pay him any mind.

"I wanted to walk around with you," Eric said. "I thought maybe we could talk to the people together."

"I'd like that, Eric." She put her arm around his waist. "Come on, Mr. Mayor, let's get our networking on."

An hour later, Linda was with him on the dance floor, swaying to a slow jam. Eric leaned down and whispered in her ear, "You're beautiful, you know that?"

Linda threw back her head and belted out a hearty laugh. "Why, Mr. Mayor, are you flirting with me?"

"If you have to ask, then I must be out of practice."

Their eyes met, and it was like a jolt of electricity. He wanted her—his wife. How or when it had happened, Eric didn't know or care. All he knew was that his heart was feeling something again for the woman in his arms, and he didn't want to let her go.

"What's on your mind, Eric?"

"You."

"It's been a long time since I was on your mind."

He stopped swaying to the music and gazed down at her. She had told him that she didn't know how to stop loving him. That had been the moment he'd started figuring out how to love her again. He hadn't wanted to admit it to himself, but it was true. "I want to move back into our bedroom. And, just in case you don't understand my meaning, I want to make love to you...tonight."

"I'll leave the light on for you," she said as she glided off the dance floor.

Eleven

Linda stretched as she opened her eyes to the dawn of a new day. There was a smile on her face as she happily noted that Eric was not only lying next to her, but his hand was around her waist, pulling her closer to him.

"Where do you think you're going?" he asked in a groggy, please-don't-leave-me kind of voice.

"To the bathroom."

"Nooo, stay with me a little while longer," he begged, holding her tighter.

"We don't have a water bed, Mr. Mayor, but if you don't let me up, we will both be floating in a minute."

He released her. "Okay, but hurry back."

She jumped out of bed. "I'll be back before you have time to miss me."

"Not true. I miss you already."

Laughing, she went into the bathroom to take care of her business, then washed her hands and face and brushed her teeth.

When she opened the door again, Eric pulled back the covers. "Come here, Woman. I want to show my appreciation for how well you handled that dinner last night."

"Oh, you've already done that; believe me."

"A man can never thank his wife enough. At least, that's what a wise woman used to tell me." He gave her a wink. "I wonder if she still believes that?"

Eric's words tugged at her heart, and she closed her eyes. When they were first married, she used to tell him that all the time. That he still remembered the good days, even after suffering with her through so many bad days, made her love him even more. She opened her eyes and smiled at him. "Oh yeah, Baby, I still believe that." And she rejoined him in bed.

Later, as they lay in each other's arms, Linda said, "I need you to do something for me."

Eric lifted her long, curly hair and kissed the back of her neck. "Ask away."

"Can you please go downstairs and make sure all of the liquor bottles from last night's dinner party have been cleared out?"

"I thought we paid a cleanup crew to handle that this afternoon."

"We did, but…."

He turned her around to face him. "What's wrong, Linda? You didn't touch the stuff last night. I finally believe that you've been cured. Why do you sound so worried about it?"

They had been having such a good time, she hated to burst his bubble. But she didn't see any way around it. "I'm an alcoholic, Baby."

He touched her nose with his fingertip. "You mean, you're a former alcoholic."

She sighed. "You and I both have to face the fact that recovering from alcoholism takes time. I don't know how long it will be before I lose the desire for the drink altogether. Last night, I had to keep praying and reminding myself of how much alcohol had taken from me, just so I wouldn't grab one of those flutes of champagne and gulp it down."

He pulled her into a tight hug. "Darien ordered the liquor. He was worried that the donors might feel slighted if they couldn't get drunk at our expense. But I promise you, it will never happen again."

"Thank you for understanding."

He got out of bed and threw on a robe. "I'll go and check things out." He started for the door, then stopped and turned around. "I'm glad you told me how hard this is for you. Whenever you need my help, just ask. We're a team, and I'll always be here for you."

Now he was sounding more like the husband she had married all those years ago. And in that moment, Linda knew that things would work out for them.

The rest of the month followed a blissful pattern of family time, fun time, and midnight lovemaking. Eric was happy again, and Linda was enjoying the fact that she was his delight once more. She only wished that she could confide in him about the group for recovering alcoholics that she had founded, but she knew that if he found out, it would be the kiss of death for their newfound love.

Still, Linda couldn't stop lending a hand and offering support to the women who came to her for help. First, there had been Susan from the gym, and then another woman, by the name of Brenda Lawson, had approached her after church one Sunday. Both Susan and Brenda knew of other women who wanted to be free from alcoholism. So, Linda had started meeting regularly with all of the women a few weeks back.

Since they didn't have the money to build an organization, Linda invited the women to her home during the afternoon, while Eric was at work. She prayed with the women and told them stories about how she'd found freedom from her own addiction. At the end of each meeting, she invited the women to accept Jesus into their lives, because Linda was convinced that He had made all the difference in her recovery.

On the last Friday in October, Linda was closing out her weekly meeting with prayer, and Kivonna had gone to the kitchen to grab the refreshments for their guests, when the front door opened. Linda heard her daughter say, "Hey, Daddy. What are you doing home so early?" Fear clenched Linda's heart.

"I took off early. Is that okay with you?"

"Of course," she answered. "I like it when you come home early."

"Where's your mom?" he asked.

"She's in the family room with her…friends," Kivonna said, trying not to spill the beans.

Linda said "Amen," and the women released one another's hands.

"Okay, ladies," she told them, "my daughter just brought in the refreshments, so please feel free to hang out…grab a glass of lemonade and some dessert. My husband just walked in, so I need to go say hello."

As she went to face Eric, her knees wobbled. She was so close to having her life back the way she wanted it; she just prayed that this one act of defiance wouldn't ruin everything for them. *Lord, please let him understand,* was her silent plea to God.

On tiptoes, she gave her husband a quick peck on the lips. "Hey, Handsome. What are you doing home so early?"

"I needed to talk to you about something." He glanced over her shoulder into the family room. "What's going on here? Who are those women?"

"Come on in and see for yourself." She grabbed his hand and led him into the family room. "You already know Susan," she said, gesturing to the woman. "Her husband is on City Council."

Eric threw on a plastic smile and extended his hand. "Oh, yes, I remember you. How's Harold doing?"

"A lot better, thanks to your wife."

Linda pulled him along before he could ask for an explanation of Susan's comment, then hurried through the rest of the introductions. "This is Mary, a friend of Susan's. This is Brenda—I met her at church—and this is her friend Terri."

Eric shook hands with each woman, but then he turned back to Linda with questioning eyes.

Linda decided to enlist her daughter's help yet again. "Kivonna, why don't you take your father to the kitchen?" She turned back to Eric and said, "I shouldn't be long. I'll join you two in the kitchen and explain everything."

"Hurry," he said, giving her the evil eye before following Kivonna out of the room.

Susan came over to Linda. "Why didn't you tell Eric about us?" she whispered.

Linda turned to the woman who had become her friend and said, "Just pray for me, okay?"

"I'm already on that, sister; you didn't even have to ask."

Linda talked with the ladies for another twenty minutes, trying to encourage them to have faith in the process and to celebrate every accomplishment—even if it was something as small as staying away from the bottle for just one day. She hoped that her husband would understand her need to be of service to these women. She also hoped she could make him see that these women helped her to stay strong and not fall back into her previous, self-destructive behavior.

After she ushered the women out of the house, she went into the kitchen to plead her case. She kissed Eric again, just because she liked the feel of his lips on hers. "Are you hungry?"

"We can eat later. I think we need to talk right now, don't you?"

Linda looked at Kivonna. "Do you have any homework to do?"

She shook her head. "I finished my homework, but I have a spelling test to study for."

"Well, you go do that so I can talk with your father."

Kivonna skipped out of the room, oblivious to the undercurrent of anger and fear drifting between her parents. Linda slowly turned back to Eric. "If you're going to yell and scream, we probably should handle this in our room."

He got up from the kitchen table and stomped up the stairs. When he was halfway up, he noticed that Linda wasn't following him. "Come on," he growled.

Sighing, she got up from the table and followed her husband. Life had been going great for her family. *God be with me.* She went upstairs, entered the bedroom, closed the door behind her, and held up a hand. "I know you're upset, but if you could please hear me out before you go off half-cocked and get us both saying things we'll regret."

"I want to say a whole lot right now, Linda, and I don't think I'll regret any of it."

"Baby, listen to me—"

"You went behind my back. When you asked me for money to start your little recovery program, I said no. What did you think— that I'd be happy about these people being in our home, because it was cost-effective?"

"You are correct. I didn't tell you that I was meeting with these women."

"Darn straight, I'm correct. I thought I could trust you, and then you go and do something like this. I just don't understand it, Linda."

"I didn't want to go behind your back, Eric, but you refused to listen. You don't seem to realize how important this is to me."

"Look, I get that you are an alcoholic. I'm trying my best to deal with that, especially since you've stopped drinking. But I didn't sign up for a marriage like this, and I sure don't want the whole world to know what we're dealing with."

She walked over to him and put her arms around him, hoping to comfort him. "My weakness has not been fair to you or Kivonna. I know that I have a great deal to make up for, but I'm getting stronger every day, and those women you met today are helping me."

He stepped away from her and sat down on the bed. A tortured look took up residence on his face.

"What's wrong, Baby?" Linda sat down next to him. "Talk to me."

He shook his head. "I don't know. I mean…you're the one with the problem, but I come off sounding like a jerk when I forbid you to help others with the same problem."

"You're not a jerk. My illness could hurt your political career. I get that. But, while you are afraid of exposure, I believe that God will make a way once we come clean."

"I've always been the responsible one in my family. I help people with issues. I don't want others to know about my issues. Is that so bad?"

She put her hand on his shoulder. "Baby, they already know. Two of the women who were in our family room today approached me for help because they noticed that I had stopped drinking. Don't you see that we can't hide our sins from the world? They'll be dug up, eventually."

Still hanging his head, Eric told her, "That's why I came home early today. I received a call from someone who said he saw the accident. He wants ten million dollars for his silence."

Linda gasped. "We don't have that kind of money."

He took her hand and gave it a squeeze. "I'm thinking about taking it from the foundation funds."

She gasped again, then stood up and backed away from her husband, shaking her head.

"There's no other way, Linda. I have to take the money."

"I know I caused this problem by driving drunk in the first place, but please don't compound it by stealing from your father. You are too good of a man for that."

"I'll do whatever it takes to protect my family."

She shook her head again. "Don't lie to yourself, Eric. If you steal that money from your father, it's not to protect me…it's to protect your political career."

"You could go to jail, Linda."

"God will make a way, Eric; we just have to put our trust in Him."

He stood up, enraged. "Lately, that's all I hear from you—'God will do this' or 'God will do that.' Where was God when you became an alcoholic, huh? Why didn't He stop you from ruining all of our lives in the first place?"

His words knocked her down and kicked her in the gut. "I…I'm sorry for what I did to you, Eric. It sounds like you want to give up and just go sign those divorce papers you threatened me with a month or so ago. But, before you do that, can you do something for me?"

He took a deep breath, appearing to calm down. "Believe it or not, Linda, I don't want to divorce you. But I don't want to be in this situation, either."

She held out her hands to him. "Come pray with me, my love."

Eric prayed with Linda that afternoon and then again before they went to bed that night. On Sunday, Linda asked him to attend church with her, and he got up and got dressed without complaint, surprising even himself. They enjoyed the service and were on a spiritual high as they stood waiting for Kivonna to finish talking with some of her friends.

Eric leaned over and whispered in Linda's ear, "The black-mailer will be calling me back tomorrow. I'll have to give him an answer."

She looked at him. "Would you mind taking a drive with me today?"

"Not at all, but where are we going?"

"I want to introduce you to someone."

"Okay, but what about this guy that I need to deal with tomorrow? What do you think we should do?"

"Schedule a press conference for tomorrow morning. Let's get this out in the open, and then, with God's help, we'll move on with our lives."

He eyed her warily.

"Do you trust me, Baby? More important, do you trust God?"

Eric thought about that for a moment. His father had raised them to believe in God. Before Eric had learned to tie his shoes, he'd known about God—known his father felt that his family had been blessed and highly favored by his God. It was high time that Eric developed the faith of his father. His wife had already been recruited by Joel Morrison, and he needed to catch up. "Yeah, Baby," he said. "I trust you and God."

Twelve

Eric sat behind his desk, tapping his fingers on the telephone he was supposed to be using to set up the press conference Linda had asked for. His wife wanted to tell the truth and take whatever punishment came her way. That was all fine and good for her, but Eric knew that making a public disclosure would not only cause her problems; it would also cripple his political aspirations.

Eric loved his wife, and he didn't want to lose her; he had finally come to terms with that. But did he love her enough to stand by her side and cover her while the chips fell on both of them? That was the question he was grappling with—and the reason his fingers were tap-dancing on the telephone receiver.

Eric had decided that he would not take money from the foundation without asking his father first. However, if his father said it was okay, Eric would rather just pay his blackmailer and put an end to the whole thing. But Linda's sense of rightness wouldn't allow her to continue living a lie. She seemed to believe that her ability to stay sober—to make her victory over alcoholism official—depended on her taking ownership for what she'd done.

Finally, he picked up the phone and punched in the number. He realized that Linda was the most important thing in the world to him, and they were a team; he would do whatever was necessary to help her stay sober, and he wouldn't jeopardize her sobriety for the sake of a governorship or even for a place in the Oval Office. Linda came first, plain and simple.

When his press secretary picked up the phone, he said, "I need to call a press conference for eleven o'clock this morning."

"What is this concerning, Mr. Mayor?" she asked.

"New information concerning the Terrell Anderson accident," Eric said, and then hung up before she could ask any more questions.

There. He'd done it. And although he'd expected to feel anxious and nervous, Eric actually leaned back in his chair and smiled. He had long known that Linda believed she came in a distant second in importance to his career. He hoped and prayed that this would show her that he had finally placed her in her rightful position. From this moment forward, Linda and Kivonna would always come first in his life.

Darien burst into Eric's office with the scowl of the devil on his face. "Are you seriously trying to ruin your chances of winning this race? Please tell me that what I just heard is incorrect."

Eric sat up. "What did you hear?"

"You're not really going to announce to the press that Linda—" Darien put his hand over his mouth and stepped backward.

"You knew, didn't you?"

Recovering, Darien removed his hand and strode toward Eric's desk. "Of course I knew. I was in the office when your gardener called you. I followed you that night to see what you would do. But when Michael took the fall...." He shrugged his shoulders. "I figured all's well that ends well, you feel me?"

"Yeah, I feel you. But there was just one problem: This thing didn't end well. I lied. I schemed." Eric laughed bitterly. "But it turns out that while I was going down a path of destruction, my wife was getting her life back together."

"That's fine—Linda is sober now," Darien said. "Why in the world would she want to destroy her life when she doesn't have to?"

"She can't live with the lies anymore. And, to tell you the truth, neither can I."

Darien rolled his eyes. "Don't act all righteous with me. If it weren't for that blackmailer, you wouldn't even consider going public with this."

Eric looked at the man who'd been his best friend since college. Darien had never had the kind of money he desired more than life itself. He'd gone to school on a scholarship and then begun working on political campaigns.

At that moment, it was as if a light had turned on in Eric's mind. "It was you, wasn't it?"

"What was me?" Darien asked, irritation edging his voice.

"You had that guy call me about the accident. Were the two of you going to split the ten million fifty-fifty?"

Darien didn't respond.

Eric stood up and pointed to the door. "You're done. Get out of here."

"You don't have a prayer of winning this election without me," Darien insisted.

"Then I guess I won't win it, because I'm done dealing with you. Now get out, before I have you thrown out."

Darien hesitated, opened his mouth to speak, then seemed to think better of it. He turned around and walked out of the office.

As Eric sat back down and tried to recover from the crushing blow, he realized that what his father had told him since he was a young man was true: Man was suspect, but he could always put his trust in God. So, at that moment, Eric decided to do just that. He would go to the press conference to support his wife, but his trust for the outcome would be in God.

⌢

The conference room was jam-packed with members of the media. Linda started sweating. She wanted to do the right thing, but seeing all of the people swarming around like vultures gave her pause. The information she was about to reveal could send her to prison and could end her husband's political career. Could their marriage survive either of those things?

Eric squeezed her hand, silently letting her know they were in this together. She glanced up at him and saw that he was smiling down at her with eyes that spoke of love and respect. She smiled back, and then he stepped to the microphone.

"Thank you all for coming here today," Eric said. "We won't keep you long, but there is a bit of relevant information concerning Terrell Anderson's accident that occurred in our city several months back that we need to clear up."

One of the side doors opened, and there was a huge commotion in the room as photographers tried to snap shots of Terrell's entrance. Linda smiled; she knew Terrell wouldn't let her down. She had taken Eric to visit him at his rehab facility the night before, and both she and Eric had told Terrell about the press conference they were planning. Terrell had agreed to attend, and Linda was now leaning on the young man for the strength she needed to do what was right.

Following Terrell into the conference room were Tawanda, Les, and Mr. and Mrs. Anderson. Linda took in a deep breath, silently praying that the Anderson family wouldn't hate her when this was over.

Terrell stepped up to the podium next to Linda, as Eric continued, "The truth of the matter is that my gardener didn't hit Terrell that night."

Cameras flashed as reporter after reporter yelled, "Then who did?"

Eric opened his mouth but said nothing. He turned to Linda. After a moment, he faced the crowd again, but still no words escaped his mouth. Linda grabbed hold of the microphone and said, "I did. Eric was at work when the entire incident occurred.

Michael Underwood wanted to help me, so he told the police that he'd been driving my car."

"Why would he do that?" a reporter asked.

Linda cleared her throat. "Because I had been drinking."

After those words, questions were coming from so many directions that Linda didn't know which one to answer first.

Terrell stepped to the podium and took the microphone. "You all need to pipe down a bit," he said. "Now, Mrs. Morrison may have been wrong for drinking and driving, but she is the one who made sure I received the proper rehabilitation. And because of that, I am now officially back on the Bengals roster."

The crowd went wild at that news. The reporters asked Terrell a few more questions about his recovery and his contract. After about five minutes of that, Eric took the microphone back from Terrell. "Thank you all again for coming," he told the crowd. "That's all we have to say for now." Then he grabbed Linda's hand and started heading for the exit.

Before they could make it out the door, a reporter stopped them. "Mr. Mayor, given that you ran for your position on a platform of integrity and honesty—reportedly the same platform you were planning for your gubernatorial run—do you expect to drop out of the race?"

Before Eric could answer, Linda said, "My husband is no quitter. Look how long he stuck it out with me." The crowd erupted into good-humored laughter, so Linda continued, "Eric Morrison has done a great deal for this city, and he plans to reduce the unemployment and foreclosure rates across Ohio, which will lead all of us to a better economic future. So, I don't think the voters of this great state will judge my husband based on the mistakes his wife has made."

"So, what should they judge him on?" a snippy reporter asked.

Linda looked up at Eric with a grateful smile and a heart overflowing with love. She turned back to the reporters and said, "If they're smart, they'll judge him for his own character, his strength, and his devotion to the State of Ohio."

"That's right!" Eric shouted, as if this were a pep rally. "Linda and I will give this race everything we've got, and then we'll let the voters decide." With that, they walked out, arm in arm, ready to do battle together—and to love each other, come what may.

Epilogue

Linda was arrested after her announcement at the press conference. But Judge Wilson took into consideration all of the glowing remarks Terrell Anderson made concerning her character, as well as everything his sister, Brenda Lawson, told him about the organization Linda had founded, and how it was helping her to recover from five years of alcohol addiction. He sentenced her to probation and community service rather than prison.

Eric Morrison didn't get a chance to run for governor. He lost in the primary, and another Democrat beat the incumbent governor. However, four years later, he became a United States Senator and served for three terms. He then went back home, ran for governor again, and won.

Now in his second term as governor of Ohio, Eric Morrison is running for president, with Linda and their four children by his side. They never quite made it to the half-dozen children they had originally wanted, but the three other children Linda birthed into the world brought them just as much joy as their big sister, Kivonna, the current mayor of Cincinnati.

Looking back on every trial and tribulation, Eric and Linda have come to realize that God never fails—that, even when it seems as if all is lost, for those who put their faith and trust in God, He works everything out in the end.

After that fateful Monday morning press conference, Eric finally understood why his father considered his family to be blessed and highly favored by God. Because Joel Morrison had done a good job of instilling Christian principles into his children when they were young, they were now coming to accept Christ, each in his or her own way. Eric just hoped that his knuckleheaded brother Shawn would soon come to know the truth. It seemed as if Shawn was heading for the hardest fall of any of the Morrison children. Still, Eric had confidence that God would be with his little brother.

The Playboy

One

Shawn Morrison, the touchdown king of the New Orleans Saints, was in the Déjà Vu Showgirls club, making it rain for two strippers named Fire and Desire. He and his boys stood at the edge of the stage, flashing dollar bills and screaming, "Come holla at ya' boy."

The strippers strutted over and picked up the dollars as if payday had come early.

"Man, I might have to get me a private show," said Shawn's teammate Joe Johnson, whom everybody called JoJo, as he slipped a dollar into Desire's unmentionables.

"Me first," Shawn said, like a giddy schoolboy.

"Haven't you had enough lap dances for a lifetime?"

When Shawn heard the voice, he immediately knew who was standing behind him. Paris Holmes was the most annoying ex-stripper turned reality-show princess he'd ever had the displeasure of sleeping with. He got a skin rash every time he was forced to have a conversation with her, so he just kept passing out dollars and hoping that Paris would fly away.

"Don't act like you don't hear me," she said, grabbing his arm and trying to turn him around.

But at six foot three, and weighing 260 pounds, Shawn was built like a linebacker, even though he was one of the best tight ends ever to play for the Saints. No mere woman could move his solid form unless he wanted to be moved.

Shawn brushed Paris's hand away. "I'm busy," he growled.

"Everybody in here can see how busy you are." With a smirk on her face, Paris added, "We can all see that you're a low-life, deadbeat daddy who'd rather spend his money on strippers than pay his child support."

Shawn turned hateful eyes onto his nemesis. He threw the dollars he had left on the floor in front of her. "That's all you're getting from me."

She laughed at him. "In your dreams, sweetheart. When the DNA comes back on Imani, you're going to need a second career to pay me off. How's your batting arm?"

"Terrible, but I won't have to worry about a baseball career, because when the DNA comes back, it's going to be 'game over.'"

A camera flashed.

"Man, you might want to lower your voice," JoJo muttered.

Another camera flashed.

"Forget that," Shawn exploded. "She wants to come in here acting all brand-new, when she knows that kid could belong to that senator or that rapper dude she used to date." He snapped his finger and added, "Or any of them suckas she was kicking it with on that nasty *Bad Girls* reality show she got thrown off of."

Paris put her hands on her hips. "Say what you want, Shawn, but I know that Imani is yours."

"The jury's still out on that one," he said. "And I'm not paying one copper penny until Mr. DNA says I have to." This wasn't Shawn's first, second, or third time at bat. To date, five women— including his brother Isaiah's ex-wife, Tanya—had claimed he was their baby's daddy. But the DNA had told the truth. He hadn't fathered any of those kids, and he was positive that he wasn't Paris's baby's daddy, either. There were only two children Shawn knew for sure were his, and they had been birthed by his ex-fiancée, the love of his life, who wouldn't give him a second chance. Actually, Shawn had been on chance number six with

Lily when she'd finally decided that enough was enough and left him.

"You're only acting this way because Lily is mad about you having another baby."

"Keep Lily's name out of your mouth," he warned her. "She don't have nothin' to do with what's going on between you and me."

"And I say she has everything to do with it, since you're taking care of her kids but won't do the same for mine."

"Is there lint between your ears or something? Did you fail an IQ test? I keep telling you that Lily's kids are my kids. I know that for a fact, so I handle my business as a father." He scrunched up his nose as if he'd smelled something foul. "But you and your kid are suspect."

Paris snarled at Shawn. "When the DNA test comes back and proves that you are the father, I'm going to take your deadbeat behind to the bank. Then you'll be making it rain in my house."

With balled fists, Shawn said, "Ooh, I wish I'd never met your conniving, trifling self."

"Oh, really? Well, you didn't say that while you were spending that weekend in Paris."

"I'll never go back, believe that. It was the worst weekend of my life. I need my head examined for fooling with a money-hungry hooker like you."

Paris slapped him.

Shawn grabbed her hand, pulling her closer, so that they were face-to-face. "Don't ever put your hands on me again. Because you won't like the lick I give back—believe that, Baby." He shoved her away from him, turned back toward the stage, grabbed a couple of bucks from JoJo's hand, and continued on with his evening, as if Paris had never interrupted him.

⌒

Lily Washington took a quick peek in the visor mirror. She had on a simple, no-name, blue jean dress that was cut off just above her knees. Since leaving Shawn, she no longer went on shopping sprees or set foot in Neiman Marcus; she made do with what she had.

Lily smiled as she looked down at her shoes. Before leaving Shawn, she'd packed up most of her collection of shoes and handbags. Today, she was rocking her Jimmy Choo mock croc pumps with matching handbag—some of the souvenirs she'd held on to.

As she stepped out of her BMW—another gift she'd kept—she almost felt guilty about all of these trappings from her old life with a man she'd truly loved and thought loved her back. But he'd turned out to be a jerk who didn't know how to come home and kept dropping his pants in the presence of other women.

Lily had been heartbroken when she'd left Shawn. But her mom had taken her to church, and it was there that Lily had finally found peace. She'd accepted the Lord Jesus Christ into her life, and He had mended her heart. "So, what are you doing going back?" she asked herself aloud.

Well, she wasn't really going back, per se. She wasn't meeting with Shawn today, but she had agreed to have brunch with some of the football wives and girlfriends she had hung around during her relationship with her cheating ex-fiancé. She had successfully avoided the women for about a year now, but there had been a recent influx of calls, and it seemed they would never let up. Lily felt bad for having ignored all those women—after all, some of them had been genuine friends. So, here she was, parked outside the sports bar where the New Orleans Saints and their groupies liked to hang out.

She took a deep breath. The second her Jimmy Choos hit the pavement, her stomach lurched, and she thought she was going to throw up the oatmeal she'd eaten for breakfast, right there in the parking lot. *You have nothing to fear*, she chided herself. *These people don't control your destiny. You don't owe anyone anything, and you don't want anything from anyone. This is just a friendly lunch with the girls.*

She kept up this mantra, putting one foot in front of the other, until she burst through the door with a confident swag most of the women in that bar and grill probably wished they could pull off. She swung her long, silky black hair to the side, then paused, running her hands through it, as she looked for her girl Cindy.

She spotted her seated in the corner, directly beneath one of the big-screen televisions that hung all around the restaurant, all of them tuned to various sports channels. Cindy waved her over. Ignoring the astonished looks on the faces of the men and women who knew her situation, Lily smiled and strode toward the table. It was the most coveted place there—the wives' club table.

Cindy stood and kissed her on the cheek. "Girl, I thought you changed your mind or something."

Grabbing a seat next to Darlene, JoJo's wife, Lily put on her fakest smile of the day.

"Hey, girl!" Darlene greeted her. "Why are you so late? We didn't think you were coming, so we put our food order in already."

"I had to get my children ready for school."

"Mmph," Darlene grunted. "That's what nannies are for."

"Well, not everyone has a nanny." Lily kept her voice quiet, nonconfrontational, but she was beginning to regret agreeing to meet these women today.

Carmen, the longtime girlfriend of one of the team's linebackers, said, "I don't know why you don't have a nanny, 'cause I know Shawn is breaking you off at least ten large every month."

With the seven thousand a month she received from Shawn, Lily tithed 10 percent to her church and paid the mortgage, the household bills, and the kids' tuition to their private school. Half of what was left went toward a college fund for her children. But none of that was Carmen's business.

"Leave her alone, Carmen," Cindy said, coming to her defense. "Lily is very thrifty. She's saving for her children's college fund."

"Well, I know that a mind is a terrible thing to waste and all," Darlene put in, "but Shawn has too much money for you to be going without because you're saving for future events."

"What if Shawn breaks a leg and can't run that ball anymore?" Lily reasoned. "Do you think the Saints will keep paying him? No, a football player's career is not promised from one game to the next, so it's my job to look after my children's future."

"Dang, girl! You are taking this 'do without, so your kids can have a future' thing a bit far," Carmen asserted. "I mean, open your eyes, Boo Boo—Shawn's father is practically a billionaire. So, if Sonny-Poo won't do right, just call on Big Daddy."

Lily didn't respond. She was too busy kicking herself for allowing these women back into her world. When she'd dumped Shawn, Lily had sworn that she would never have anything else to do with any of the "trophy wives" Shawn had insisted that she spend her time with.

The server came to the table to take Lily's order.

"Just a glass of orange juice, please," Lily said.

When the server walked away, Lily turned to Cindy, hoping to get this show on the road so she could get out of here. "So, why did you ask to see me this morning?"

Just above Lily's head, the sixty-four-inch television screen switched to a deodorant commercial, and Lily had to close her eyes as Shawn's sexy, caramel-chocolate self strutted onto the screen, wearing a pair of shorts and nothing else. His broad, muscular chest and sinewy arms were in full view for any and every woman who wanted to lust after him. But Lily was through with all that.

"Girl, open your eyes." Darlene shook her shoulder. "That man can't jump through the television screen."

Feeling foolish at being caught in such an awkward moment, Lily opened her eyes. It was at that moment that Shawn lifted the deodorant stick and gave the camera his deep-dimpled smile. She wanted to close her eyes again and block him out of her life. It wasn't fair that Shawn Morrison was so gorgeous and so evil at the same time. God should give every evil person warts and a beer belly. And there should be a sign tacked to the back of his shirt that said, "Stay away from this ugly critter."

Unfortunately, Lily knew, evil comes in all packages. She massaged her temples, knowing she wasn't being fair. Shawn was the father of her children, and she had stayed with him for five years. There was no way she would have done that if the man had been pure evil. So, maybe he wasn't evil…but what he had done to her heart had been.

"Lily, girl, we aren't trying to stress you out," Cindy told her. "The girls and I just wanted to talk to you about a business venture that's been presented to us."

The server returned to distribute the women's meals. After handing Lily her orange juice, she turned and left.

Lily took a sip of her juice. "What type of venture? And what does it have to do with me?"

"Well," Cindy began—evidently she had been dubbed spokesperson—"we've been in talks with a producer who wants to film a football wives show with us, here in Louisiana."

The excitement in Cindy's voice couldn't be missed, but Lily was confused. "Okay, but what does that have to do with me?"

As she asked the question, the door to the restaurant opened, and in walked Paris Holmes, the last person Lily wanted to see. She turned her attention back to the women at the table, hoping that Paris wouldn't notice her and feel the need to torment her, as usual.

"Duh!" Darlene said. "You and Shawn were together for years."

"Yeah, but I never married him. I never was, nor am I now, a 'football wife.'"

Paris slammed her Coach purse down on the table and sat down next to Cindy. "I never married him, either, but we both have babies by the hound dog, so why shouldn't we earn a little money off of that?"

"I don't profit off of my children." Lily stood up, fished three dollars out of her purse, and placed them on the table. Then she turned cold eyes on Cindy. "If this was the only reason you invited me here today, please don't bother calling again." With that, she turned and walked out of the restaurant.

As far as Lily was concerned, those women had an overinflated sense of importance, and she wanted nothing to do with them or their drama-filled reality show. She didn't even like the slew of reality shows currently airing on TV. They were filled with such nonsense and filth that she was ashamed for the people featured on them. And then, her so-called friends had had the nerve to invite Paris Holmes to meet them for brunch, when they had to know that Lily did not want to see another woman who claimed to have had a child by Shawn.

"Lily, wait up."

Lily turned to see Paris jogging toward her. She ignored her and continued toward her car. But Lily didn't move fast enough, because Paris caught up with her as she was opening her car door.

"Let's be adult about this, Lily."

"What do you want, Paris? I have things to do." She actually had the next two hours free, but "things to do" could include getting in her car and driving away from the nightmare she had stepped into.

"This won't take long. I just need for you to understand that everyone is counting on you. I worked long and hard trying to get Jason Brooks to produce this show. He's on board, but he thinks the added drama of you and me trying to deal with Shawn and each other would give the show the extra 'something something' that it needs to be a hit."

God help her, Lily wanted to hit this woman. She took a deep breath. "As I said before, I have things to do."

"Who do you think you are?" Paris exploded. "You're no better than me. You got caught up with a baby's daddy, just like I did. You're not special, so stop trying to act like your stuff don't stink."

"Get out of my face," Lily warned her.

"And if I don't?"

Lord Jesus, I really want to do this woman harm, but I don't want to go to jail, so I need You to help me, she silently prayed, calling on the One who had seen her through her breakup with Shawn and so many other tribulations along the way.

"Is everything okay over there?" shouted Seth, the restaurant owner, leaning out the front door.

Lily used that opportunity to get in her car and drive off. As she pulled out of the lot, she picked up her cell phone and called her baby's daddy.

Shawn picked up on the first ring. "Hey, Baby. What's up?"

"Don't call me 'Baby'!" she yelled.

"What's wrong? What happened?" Shawn asked, immediately sounding alert.

"Paris Holmes happened. And I'm sick of your little girlfriend approaching me. I'm telling you now, Shawn, if you don't handle her, I will."

"I don't have nothing to do with that crazy chick."

"Whatever, Shawn. Just tell all of your girlfriends to leave me alone." Lily hung up, and the tears that she'd promised herself would never be shed over Shawn again traitorously poured down her face.

Two

"Hey, Shawn. What you know? Good?" asked the woman clad in a white spandex jumpsuit that clung so tight, every person who met her felt as if he knew her intimately.

Shawn had known the hazel-eyed beauty in the most intimate way possible. He had dated Jules Moore before he met Lily. She'd been cool people, but once he'd gotten to know Lily and had moved her into his house, he hadn't wanted anything to do with other women. So, he'd lost touch with Jules. Now that Lily wouldn't listen to the truth and wanted nothing to do with him, Shawn saw no reason why he should act like a good little choir boy. "I haven't seen you in a while. Where you been hiding?"

Jules flashed him a smile that made most men want to pay her rent. "I'm not the one who's been hiding. If I remember correctly, you came to me with lovesick starry eyes and told me that you were getting married and couldn't hang out with me anymore."

Shawn shrugged his shoulders. "Things change."

"Tell me about it," Jules said. "Me and my man just broke up, too."

"So, you might need a night on the town to get your mind off that sucka, huh?"

"Something like that," Jules said. He could tell that the nonchalance in her tone was forced.

Shawn hoisted his duffel bag onto his shoulder and pointed toward the stadium. "I've got to get in there and handle my business, but I'll give you a call after practice and set something up." He walked away feeling good about the smile that he'd left on Jules's face. But then he thought about the way Lily used to smile at him, and found himself wishing he could see that again.

Shawn was running his last scrimmage when trouble descended on him. Tito, their biggest linebacker, was trying to block him. Shawn misstepped, Tito tackled him, and then Shawn went down on the same knee that had been giving him trouble since his first year as a pro. He let out an expletive as he lay on the field, holding his knee, wondering why life kept turning sour on him.

"You all right?" Tito asked, standing over him.

"Naw, man, I'm hit. Tell them to get the stretcher. I don't want to walk on it."

They brought the stretcher and carried Shawn to the locker room, where Dr. Hank was working on Roy Carter, the team's wide receiver and all-around do-gooder of the year. He was the type of player who got on his knee and crossed himself with his head lowered in praise to God after making a touchdown. Shawn steered clear of him.

"Let me go get some pain meds for the both of you," Dr. Hank said. "I think I might need to get a few X-rays, too." He stepped out of the room.

"Hey, Shawn," Roy said, wearing a huge smile.

"Hey, Roy." Shawn returned the greeting without so much as a grin.

"I just learned about an organization that lets people purchase desks for schoolchildren in Malawi," Roy told him. "You might want to check it out. There's a Web site that makes donating really easy."

Here we go with the do-gooder trash. "Man, are you trying to tell me that school kids in Hawaii don't have desks?"

"Not Maui—*Malawi*. In Africa. Those poor kids have to sit on the floor, holding paper and pencils in their hands, trying to do their schoolwork." Roy shrugged. "I just thought you might be interested, since you're starting that foundation for your dad and all."

Dr. Hank came back in the room and dispensed painkillers to both players. Once Shawn had swallowed his meds, he sat up and hung his legs over the side of the bed. "Look, man," he said to Roy. "I don't really believe in all that 'Give, and it shall be given back to you' stuff that my daddy's on."

"But your father gave you the money, so you might as well use it to do good, right? And those kids could really use your help. I made a contribution just last night."

"I gave the money back to my daddy. I'm just not a do-gooder like you."

"I didn't know you'd given the money back." Roy sounded disheartened.

"What? Please. I told the old man that if he wanted to put some paper in my hands, then I needed it to come with no strings attached. I mean, look at me. My knee is all busted up. Who's to say how many more years I have before I have to retire? That was supposed to be my money, and he wants to just give it away. Fine. He can do it without me. I'm not with it."

"I'm sorry you feel that way, but I think you passed on an opportunity to make a real difference in the lives of others."

Shawn shrugged. "Forget the world and all its occupants. I'm still waiting on someone to make a difference in my life."

After that lovely speech, Shawn and Roy were taken to X-ray. Roy didn't bother Shawn again; however, Shawn could feel the man's disapproval. But Shawn didn't care. He wasn't about to spend his life pretending that he was in love with the idea of giving away money that should have been put in his pockets. He wasn't made like that, and his daddy—the great and wonderful Joel Morrison—should know that by now.

After the X-ray, Shawn limped his way toward his pure black Mercedes-Benz SLR McLaren with light brown Napa leather interior. As he reached for the door handle, a man and a woman dressed in suits walked up to him. "Shawn Morrison?" the man said.

As if he doesn't know. "The one and only."

"I'm Detective Ron Jones, and this is my partner, Marcie Henderson." Detective Jones pointed to the woman standing next to him. The looks on their faces were all business.

"What can I do for you?" Shawn asked.

"We need to speak with you down at the station," Detective Jones said. "It's regarding Paris Holmes."

Shawn opened his car door and threw his duffel bag in. "I don't need to come to the station. This'll be a quick conversation, because I don't have anything to say about Paris. I'll let my lawyers deal with her in court."

"Your lawyers won't be dealing with Ms. Holmes," Detective Henderson said quickly.

"Oh, trust me; I keep a guy on retainer to handle groupies like Paris. I'm not worried."

"What Detective Henderson is trying to tell you," Detective Jones said tersely, "is that Paris Holmes is dead."

Three

Hey, Isaiah. What are you doing?"

Isaiah rubbed his eyes and glanced at the clock on his night-stand. "It's five in the morning, Eric," he hissed into the phone. "What do you think I'm doing?"

Eric took a deep breath. "I'm sorry for waking you up so early, but I need your help."

On full alert now, Isaiah sat up. "Is Linda all right?" His sister-in-law was a recovering alcoholic, and Isaiah and his wife, Ramona, had been praying fervently for her, especially since she was now pregnant.

"No, nothing's wrong with Linda. At least, not in the way you might be thinking."

"Well then, why would you call me at five in the morning?" Isaiah felt a surge of panic. He had talked to his father just last night, and the man had seemed in good spirits and health, but he would turn eighty-five in a few months. "Did something happen to Dad?"

"Isaiah, will you please calm down and let me tell you what's going on?"

Ramona pushed Isaiah and pointed at the door. "I'm trying to sleep," she said groggily.

Isaiah got out of bed and carried the cordless phone across the hall into his home office.

"One of us needs to get down to Louisiana and help Shawn before Dad finds out what's going on," Eric said.

Isaiah rolled his eyes heavenward. His younger brother was always getting himself into some kind of trouble, with the rest of the family always coming to his rescue without question. But Isaiah was through with that routine. After learning that the brother he'd trusted had slept with his ex-wife before he'd married her, Isaiah was done. "What has Shawn gotten himself into now, and why do we have to help him?"

"The latest woman who accused him of fathering her child was found stabbed to death, and the police have taken Shawn in for questioning."

"And?" Isaiah asked, figuring that there had to be more to this story. If all the police were doing was questioning Shawn, why did they need to be concerned?

"Shawn isn't cooperating," Eric answered.

"That figures. Well, if that bonehead won't help the police find the killer of the mother of one of his kids, why should we lift a finger to help him?"

"I don't know what's going through Shawn's mind right now, but I'm worried that if he gets arrested, and word gets back to Daddy…I'm not sure his heart can take something like this."

Put that way, Eric made a compelling case. "Okay, you're right," Isaiah finally said. "So, what do we need to do to help this knucklehead?"

Eric hesitated a moment. "One of us needs to go down there and talk some sense into Shawn."

"What are you calling *me* for?" Isaiah groused. He was not in the mood to see Shawn. Two years had passed since discovering his brother's treachery, and Isaiah had been praying earnestly for the ability to forgive him. While he'd made great progress, so far, his heart still wasn't fully in the forgiving business—not where Shawn was concerned.

"Linda's doctor just put her on bed rest," Eric explained. "After having those three miscarriages years ago, she's nervous about being on bed rest. I can't leave her right now. You understand that, don't you, Isaiah?"

He did understand, because he knew it was those miscarriages that had caused Linda's drinking problem in the first place. And Isaiah knew that he wouldn't leave Ramona if she were six months pregnant and had just been put on bed rest.

"Why don't you call Dee Dee?" Isaiah suggested. "She could go down there and knock some sense into Shawn's thick head."

"Dee Dee's shooting a film in Italy right now. Drake and Natua are over there with her."

Elaine and her husband were on a mission trip in Mexico, so they wouldn't be able to go, either. Isaiah wished he had some good excuse to bail out, like his sisters, but he didn't. So, he lowered his head, said a quick prayer, and then told Eric, "Let me talk to Ramona, to make sure she and Erin will be okay with my being gone for a day or so, and then I'll make my flight arrangements."

"I knew I could count on you, Bro. Thanks for helping out."

"Don't thank me; you and Shawn need to be thanking God, because if I wasn't 'sho nuff' saved, I'd leave that boy to fend for himself."

"Well then, praise the Lord!" Eric shouted.

"Oh—and, Eric? I don't know if I expressed this clearly enough to you last week, but Ramona and I thought you should have won the race."

"Don't worry about it, Bro. I didn't get to be governor, but I did get my family back, and that means more to me than any political office. Besides, Linda and I are already working on our strategy for my next campaign."

Isaiah shook his head. "Just don't go into Congress. You know those nutcases have an approval rating of only nine percent or so."

⌒

"Look, Shawn. We can do this the easy way or the hard way. The question is, how bad do you want to play in the next game?"

Shawn stared at the wall. He had been held in this interrogation room so long that he'd lost track of time. But that didn't matter. They could keep him in this room for a year or more, and he still wouldn't tell them anything about the day Paris was found murdered.

"I don't have anything to say to you," he finally told Detective Jones. "If you're going to arrest me, then bring on the handcuffs."

"We already know that you went to see Paris the day she was murdered. The apartment complex had a surveillance tape. We saw you coming and going. You were mad going in, but whatever that woman said to you inside her apartment just got you hotter, because smoke was basically blowing out of your ears when you left."

Shawn still said nothing.

"Paris was stabbed numerous times," Detective Henderson continued. "This was obviously a crime of passion. The only reason we haven't arrested you yet is because that same surveillance tape shows Paris leaving her apartment about an hour after you stormed out. So, what happened? Did you call and ask her to meet you somewhere? The woman was trying to take your money for that kid she just had—it's understandable that you would be upset."

There was a knock on the door, and Detective Jones opened it. "Can I help you?"

A man in a brown pinstriped suit stepped in and set his briefcase on the table. He held out his hand to Shawn. "I'm Melvin Cotrell." He turned to Detective Jones. "I have been hired to represent Mr. Morrison, and I need to know why you decided to detain my client for over thirty-six hours."

"I-I wouldn't say that we 'detained' him," Detective Jones stammered. "We've been trying to get Shawn to answer a few questions so we can find the person who killed the mother of his child. But he isn't interested in helping us, which causes me to wonder why."

"You can do all the wondering you want, but if my client isn't being charged with anything, then we are leaving this instant." Melvin Cotrell took out a business card and handed it to Jones. "The next time you'd like to have a chat with Mr. Morrison, please notify me first."

Melvin put his hand on Shawn's shoulder and directed him to stand up.

"Don't get lost, Morrison. I may need to speak with you again about this," Detective Jones said as Shawn followed his attorney out of the interrogation room.

For the first time in thirty-six hours, Shawn smiled. "Did you see the look on his face? That was priceless. Man, who hired you? My dad?"

Melvin shook his head. "Your father doesn't know anything about this, and I've been instructed to keep it that way. We are going out the back door, to avoid any nosy reporters. Come with me."

Shawn's knee was still bothering him, but he limped along after Melvin through the police station. "If my father didn't send you, who did?"

Melvin led him out the back door and toward a black sedan with tinted windows that was parked nearby. "Your brother," Melvin said, opening the back door and motioning for Shawn to get in.

All Shawn could think of was the lecture he was about to get from Eric, Mr. Do-the-right-thing. "How did Eric find out the police had me hemmed up?"

Isaiah poked his head out of the car. "Boy, quit all the yapping and get your bonehead self in this car."

The shock of seeing Isaiah caused Shawn to lose his balance. He went tumbling down, landing on his injured knee.

Isaiah jumped out of the car and helped Shawn up. "Are you all right? What happened?"

"I'm all right. I guess I was just stunned to see you." Shawn attempted to walk, but his knee caved in on him. "Not again," he muttered, without thinking.

"Not again, what?" Isaiah asked.

"Nothing. It's cool."

Melvin and Isaiah helped Shawn get into the car. As Melvin drove, Shawn focused on inhaling and exhaling, as if that would relieve his pain.

"Sorry for yelling at you, Bro." Isaiah sounded like he meant it. "I certainly didn't want you to injure yourself."

"Don't worry about it. Maybe if I'm injured so badly that I can't play anymore, you'll consider us even." But, even as Shawn said the words, he knew in his heart that nothing Isaiah might do to him could take away the sting of what he'd done to Isaiah.

Shawn had a lifetime of regrets. He just didn't know if he had enough time to make up for any of his transgressions. But he had at least started paying Lily back for all that he'd done to her, by keeping his mouth shut in the interrogation room.

Four

Rushing around the house like a madwoman, Lily got her kids dressed, packed their lunches, and called Shawn in fifteen-minute intervals. When it became obvious that he wasn't going to answer his home or cell phone, Lily called her hairstylist, Barbara.

"Hey, girl. What's up?" Barbara asked.

"Sorry to be such a flake, but I need to cancel my appointment for this morning."

"Daddy-O never showed up, huh?"

Barbara had been doing Lily's hair for ten years, so she'd been around for the entire seven years of Shawn-drama. And Lily had simply stopped pretending that all was right in her world. "He was supposed to have the boys today, but I haven't heard from him. And Shawnee has peewee football practice in forty-five minutes."

"He's normally pretty good about his weekends with the boys, isn't he?"

"Yeah, I've always been able to count on him when it came to the kids. But things change, and I'm not about to disappoint my children just because Shawn has forgotten that he's a daddy today."

"I hear you, girl. So, do you want to come in on Tuesday?"

Since she'd started attending church with her mother, Lily had been getting her hair done on Saturdays so that it would be fresh for the Sunday service. But, as Judge Judy told the countless women who came on her court show complaining about some guy who'd done them wrong, "You picked him!" Lily had not only picked Shawn Morrison; she'd done everything but shine his shoes in order to get him to notice her. And since she was now doing this salvation thing with Jesus, she had been spending a lot of time telling herself the truth as she saw it. So, she'd had to admit that she'd gotten pregnant with her first son as an attempt to keep Shawn Morrison in her life.

She wouldn't trade her children for anything, but there were days she wished she could trade in their sorry excuse for a dad for a better model. "Yeah, Barbara, I'll be in on Tuesday." She hung up the phone, swept her hair into a ponytail, and then, exhaling a sigh, headed for her sons' room to tell Shawnee and Isaiah that Mommy would be taking them to football practice today.

"Where's Daddy?" Shawnee asked the moment she opened the door.

"I don't know," Lily answered truthfully.

"But he said he would pick us up," Isaiah whined.

"I'm sorry, boys, but I can't reach your father. We need to get going if you want to be on time for practice."

Shawnee stomped his foot and folded his arms across his chest. "I don't want to go to football practice with a girl."

"Look, Boy, do you want to go to your practice or not?" Lily hated losing her temper with her children, but they were treating her like mommies didn't matter, and she simply wasn't having that—not when she'd gone through nine hours of hard labor pushing Shawnee's big head out of her too-small birth canal. She wasn't about to let her kids treat her like some second-rate parent. "I'm going to the car. If you're not there in two seconds, practice will be cancelled for you." She spun around and marched out of the room.

No, she was not about to be played like that by some five-(almost six)-year-old and his little three-year-old cosigning younger brother. *Mommy's here, and Daddy's not. Deal with it.*

Seconds later, her boys came running down the hall, nearly colliding with her as she began to descend the stairs. "I didn't mean to hurt your feelings, Mommy," Shawnee said. "If Daddy can't go, then we want you to take us."

Lily smiled at her boys. She still came in second, but who could blame them? Their father was a football superstar in this town, and she was just their mom. She put her arms around her boys as they walked down the steps. "I'm proud to be a stand-in for your father. Come on, let's go." *Rah-rah and all that.*

She grabbed her keys off the table in the foyer and hoisted her purse over her shoulder. When she opened the front door, a woman with a three-toned dye job was standing there. The hair was blond on the tips, reddish-orange in the middle and brown at the roots, but that wasn't the only thing Lily noticed. The woman was holding a baby carrier.

"I guess you're happy Paris won't be bothering you anymore," the woman said with a scornful frown.

"Excuse me? Who are you?"

"I'm Vivi, Paris's best friend. And this right here"—Vivi held out the baby carrier—"is now your responsibility."

Lily turned to her boys. "Go sit down in the living room. Mommy needs to talk to this woman for a minute." When the boys had gone, Lily turned back to Vivi. "I don't know what kind of game you and Paris are playing, but I'm not about to take this baby."

"Paris ain't playing no games. She's dead. Shawn Morrison killed her."

"What did you say?"

"You heard me. The police have that no-good dog in custody, and I hope they keep him there." Vivi put the baby carrier on the floor in front of Lily, turned on her heels, and strutted off.

"Hey, wait a minute. You can't just leave this baby with me."

She spun around. "You wanna bet? Paris don't have no family. But since you're Shawn's other baby mama, I figured you'd want to keep the family together." The crazy lady opened the door of her 90s model Ford Taurus. "I don't care what you do. I've got my own mouths to feed." Then she got in the car and sped off without so much as a backward glance.

Lily's hand flew to her mouth as she recalled the hysterical phone call she had made to Shawn just three days ago. He and Paris had become her enemies, but she never would have wished the girl dead, nor would she have wanted Shawn to be blamed for something she knew with certainty he hadn't done.

⁓

"Okay, we need to talk," Isaiah told Shawn as he followed him into his three-million-dollar home. Shawn moved slowly, supported by the pair of crutches he'd dug out of his garage.

"I need to get some sleep, Isaiah. Can't we talk about all this later?" Shawn halted in the entryway and waved his hand to indicate the expanse of his house. "Mi casa es su casa. You can have the master bedroom. I'm sleeping down here in the guest bedroom until my knee heals."

"That's all well and good, but we still need to talk." Isaiah followed him into the guest bedroom. "You're holding out on the police, and I want to know why."

Shawn sat on the bed, propping his crutches against the wall. He scrunched up his nose. "How do you know I'm holding out on the police? Matter of fact, how did you know that the police were questioning me in the first place?"

"One of Eric's college buddies works in that station. He called Eric and let him know what was going on."

"Big Brother is always watching," Shawn muttered, shaking his head in disgust.

"You should be glad somebody's been watching out for your sorry behind. Do you know what this will do to Daddy if he finds out that the police think you had something to do with that young woman's death?"

That shut Shawn up for a moment. He rubbed his hand across his mouth and then looked at Isaiah. "I didn't kill Paris. And I agree with you about Dad—I don't want him hearing anything about this. I just can't talk to the police...not yet, anyway."

"Why not, Shawn? This woman was the mother of one of your children. Why wouldn't you want to help the police find out who killed her?"

Because it might have been the mother of my other children. "I have my reasons."

Isaiah threw up his hands. "I don't even know why I left my family to come down here to see about you. Same ol' Shawn."

"What's that supposed to mean?"

"It is what it is. You hurt the people who love you the most, and you couldn't care less what happens to people once you're done with them."

Outraged, Shawn jumped to his feet. He immediately regretted his action, for his knee buckled, and pain shot through his body. He fell back on the bed and lay down, sucking in air and blowing it out. "Go home, Isaiah. You don't want to be here anyway. Just leave me alone."

Isaiah closed his eyes for a moment, as if in prayer, and then walked over to the bed and put his hand on Shawn's shoulder. "Look, I'm sorry. I didn't mean to make you hurt yourself again. But I really need you to think about our family and make the right decision."

"I am thinking about my family," Shawn said through clenched teeth. Once the pain subsided, he added, "I've made a lot of mistakes in my life, but my family is very important to me...and that includes Lily, Shawnee, and little Isaiah."

Isaiah raised his eyebrows. "Does Lily have something to do with this? Is that why you didn't want to talk to the police?"

Shawn didn't want to answer that. His mind drifted back to the two latest phone calls Lily had made to him—how upset she'd been over something Paris had done. The first time, Paris had tried to get Lily involved in some whacked-out reality show. And then, weeks later, Paris had called Lily when the results of the DNA test on Imani had come in. She'd told Lily that she didn't need her help to get the green light for the reality show about football wives, because she was officially the proud parent of one of Shawn Morrison's children.

Lily had been hysterical when she'd called him. "If you don't do something about that woman, I'm going to end up in jail because I'm going to hurt her," she'd said. Those words haunted Shawn now, because he knew that if anyone found out that he'd gone to see Paris because Lily had threatened to harm her, it would not look good for Lily. And Shawn would give up his football career and go to prison himself before he allowed the woman he loved to spend one night in jail just because he had a zipper problem.

The worst thing about the entire ordeal was that if he hadn't been so upset and distraught after Lily had broken up with him, and if his brother hadn't found out about the brief affair he'd had with Tanya, now Isaiah's ex-wife, when the two of them were still dating, then Shawn never would have gotten involved with Paris Holmes in the first place.

"Did you hear me, Shawn?"

"Huh?" Shawn's mind jolted back to the here and now.

"Does Lily have anything to do with what happened to Paris?"

Shawn opened his mouth, ready to deny, deny, deny. But somebody started leaning on his doorbell.

"What in the world?" Isaiah said.

"Probably some groupie. I'm going to take a couple more pain pills and go to sleep."

"All right. I'll see who's at the door, and then I'm going to take a nap myself. But we are not finished with this conversation."

After Isaiah let her in and told her where Shawn was, Lily headed with purposeful strides toward the guest bedroom, with the boys following behind her. When she entered, Shawn was swallowing down some pills. She lifted up the baby carrier. "I brought you something."

Evidently the pills were taking effect. Shawn slumped drowsily onto the bed and pulled the covers over his body. "Let's talk later, Lily. I messed up my knee again today and need to get some sleep."

"Daddy! Daddy!" The boys rushed into the room and jumped on the bed.

"Boys, calm down," Lily warned them. "Your daddy's been injured."

"Is that why you didn't take us to practice today?" Shawnee asked, leaning against the bed.

"Huh? Practice?" Shawn's eyes were glazing over.

"What kind of pain pills did you take?" She picked up the pill bottle from the nightstand and immediately understood why Shawn was drifting off so quickly. The one time she'd been given Percocet, she'd been out before her head hit the pillow. She set the pill bottle back down. "Come on, boys. Daddy needs to get some rest."

"But Mom, we haven't talked to Daddy all day," Shawnee moaned.

"No Daddy talk," Isaiah echoed, shaking his head.

"We don't have to leave just yet. You boys go play in the family room. We'll be here when Daddy wakes up."

Shawn's hand brushed hers. "Thanks." And then he rolled over and started snoring.

She walked out of the bedroom, following her sons, who were running through the house like madmen. She was carrying around a baby that didn't belong to her and wondering if she was about to play the fool for Shawn Morrison once again.

Five

"How are you holding up, Lily?" Isaiah asked her.

They were in the family room, lounging on Shawn's monstrous sectional, watching reruns of *Welcome to Sweetie Pie's* on OWN. Lily was rubbing Imani's back, trying to get the baby to burp.

"Not too good, seeing as how I just changed and fed a baby that belongs to my ex."

"I hear you, but at least women don't have to worry about some man trying to deceive them into believing a baby is theirs when it's not." He shook his head, and Lily realized he was referring to the painful discovery that his precious daughter, Erin, was not his biological child.

"I was sorry to hear about all the drama that went on over Erin, Isaiah. I know that Shawn was sick over everything that happened. And I have no business taking up for him, especially since I'm holding his new baby. But he truly regrets doing that to you."

Isaiah leaned against the cushiony back of the couch. "The thing that bugs me most is that, as a preacher, I talk to people about forgiveness all the time. But it has taken two years for me to come to terms with what Shawn did to me."

"I'm no preacher," Lily said, watching her children play in a far corner of the room, "but I am a child of God, and I still haven't come to terms with all the mess Shawn has put me through."

Isaiah smiled at his nephews. "They remind me of myself and Shawn at those ages." He chuckled. "I was Shawn's hero. He was always underfoot, trying to see what I was doing, so that he could copy it. And I loved looking out for him. But then Shawn grew up and became his own hero." He shook his head. "I will admit that the journey toward forgiveness came a little easier once I learned that Shawn wasn't Erin's father. The fact that I don't feel any differently toward my daughter now than when I thought she was biologically mine also seems to help."

Lily nodded. "I'm glad your love for Erin hasn't changed. That would have been an awful blow for a young child to deal with."

"Erin knows that she is my special love. And now, Erin and I have Ramona. And, let me tell you, that woman has more love in her than I could acquire in a lifetime. But enough about me. I hear that you've joined a church down here."

With a smile that came from way down deep, she said, "All I can say is, thank You, Jesus, for mothers who love the Lord. Ruth Ann had my back while I was going through all that drama with Shawn. She kept praying for me and inviting me to church. Finally, one Sunday, I just went. My life hasn't been the same since."

"I'm glad to hear it. Now, if only we could get my knuckleheaded brother to see the truth, then my visit will not have been in vain."

They watched television for a while longer, and then Isaiah played with the boys while Lily put Imani to sleep. When Isaiah returned to the couch, he looked at his watch. "How long is that boy going to sleep?"

"Considering the pain pills he took, I'd say he'll be up in about an hour or so."

"He's been asleep for almost four hours now. I need to catch a plane out of here tonight. I'm scheduled to preach the sermon tomorrow."

"I'm sure Shawn will understand if you need to leave. And don't worry—I won't kill your brother while he's sleeping."

Isaiah laughed. "That's the least of my worries, but I can't leave without talking to Shawn. It's as if the bonehead is trying to ruin his life. And that would simply destroy my father."

"What has he done now? I mean, besides having a baby by some woman who has gotten herself killed." Lily shivered at those words. "I'll admit that I didn't like Paris Holmes one bit. But I wouldn't wish death on her or anyone else."

"I know; it's really tragic. You'd think that Shawn would want to help the police find the person responsible for this woman's death, but he has flat out refused to even talk to them."

"What kind of information are they trying to get out of him?"

Isaiah hesitated for a moment. "Apparently, the police have him on surveillance tape going in and out of Paris's apartment the day she died. They said he looked angry both coming and going."

"Don't tell me they really think Shawn killed that woman!" Lily's throat tightened at the memory of what Vivi had said when she'd left Imani on her doorstep.

"Thankfully, the surveillance tape also shows Paris leaving her apartment about an hour after Shawn stormed away. So, they don't believe Shawn killed her—not at her apartment, anyway. The problem is that Shawn won't tell them why he went to Paris's. He's making himself look guilty for no reason."

Lily shook her head, sorrow filling her. "This might be my fault."

Isaiah eyed her. "I thought this might have something to do with you. Before Shawn went to sleep, he said something about family meaning everything to him…and that included you and the boys."

"I just wish we had meant that much to him when it counted."

"Men are slow sometimes." Isaiah shrugged, then looked Lily in the eye. "What does Paris's death have to do with you?"

"Nothing." Lily lifted her hands. "I promise, I had nothing to do with that woman's death. But I'm the reason Shawn went to see her." She looked down. "She called my house the other day, gloating about the DNA test results she'd just gotten." She closed her eyes, trying to shake off the memory, then refocused on Isaiah. "I called Shawn and told him that if he didn't do something about that woman, then I was going to hurt her. But I didn't mean it."

"That's why he won't talk to the police."

"But I was just talking smack—honest."

"Talking smack or not, Shawn is afraid that if he tells the police that he went to see Paris because you were angry about Imani being his child, the police might start sniffing around you, too."

"Poor Shawn. He probably thinks that he's getting ready to be a full-time dad, not just to Imani but to all three of his children." She started to laugh, but as she glanced over at Imani's sleeping form, she remembered that the reason Shawn would have custody of his daughter was because her mother was dead—and that was no laughing matter.

Isaiah's cell phone rang. He fished it out of his pocket and checked the caller ID. "It's Ramona. I need to take this."

"Go right ahead," Lily told him. "Just hand me the remote."

He passed the remote to Lily on his way out of the room. "Hey, Baby. What's going on? You missing me already?"

Lily smiled as she changed the channel to a cooking show. Her love affair with Shawn hadn't worked out, but she was always happy to hear the sound of love in the voices of other people. As she watched a chef chop this and stuff that, she caught bits and pieces of Isaiah's conversation.

He and his wife were discussing the foundation that he'd set up. Lily thought that the members of the Morrison family were doing God's work on earth, selflessly giving up their birthright so that others could receive assistance. Shawn had been the only holdout in the family. She simply didn't understand why he would refuse to help the needy, especially when he had so much to offer.

Isaiah came back to the living room. "Sorry about that. Ramona likes to run her ideas by me before making a final decision on which charities to support."

"I think what you are doing to help others is a wonderful thing," Lily told him. "I just don't understand why Shawn would refuse to do the same."

"I haven't been in a giving mood since the day you left me." Shawn hobbled into the room with just one crutch under his left arm. He sat down on the sectional with the baby between him and Lily. "So, if you want me to do this wonderful thing, I suggest you come back home where you belong."

Six

Isaiah and Lily spent half an hour convincing Shawn that Lily hadn't had anything to do with Paris's death. They then spent another hour trying to get him to agree to go back to the police station and tell them everything that occurred on the day Paris was murdered. The holdup on the agreement was not because Shawn didn't want to provide any and all evidence necessary to find the person who killed Paris; but, now that he was positive Lily hadn't been involved, he wanted to milk this thing a little while longer.

The agreement took place once Lily agreed to stay at his house and help him with the baby for three days—just long enough to give his knee a chance to heal. Shawn was also hoping that three days would be long enough for him to convince Lily that he was a changed man.

Isaiah stood up. "I'll call Melvin Cotrell and ask him to arrange a meeting with Detective Jones so you can help him with the investigation."

"Thanks, man. Just see if they can come to the house tomorrow afternoon."

"I'll make sure that Melvin informs Detective Jones of your injured knee." Isaiah then walked toward the front door, with Shawn trailing him on the crutch. When Isaiah reached the door, he turned around. "So, will we see you at Daddy's eighty-fifth birthday party next week?"

"Are you saying you actually want me there?" Shawn scoffed. "When I showed up at Elaine's birthday party, you acted like I'd stolen something from you."

"You had," Isaiah said, but he didn't raise his voice.

Shawn lowered his head. "I'm sorry about that, Bro. I was young and stupid. But I never thought you were going to marry her. If I could take it back, I would, in a heartbeat."

Shawn and Isaiah used to be very close. When he couldn't turn to anyone else in his family, Shawn had always been able to tell Isaiah about the things that concerned him. That summer when he'd come home for a visit during his senior year in college, Shawn had wanted to tell Isaiah that his girl kept coming on to him. But somehow, loyalty had gotten displaced by youthful lust.

If nothing else, Paris's dying so young had taught him that life was too short to leave things unsaid or undone. Shawn was now more determined than ever to redeem himself with Isaiah and Lily.

When Shawn lifted his eyes to his brother's, ready to plead his case, tears were streaming down Isaiah's face, which made Shawn feel even worse. This was his big brother, a man Shawn had always revered for his convictions and his strength; and he was standing in his foyer, crying.

"I never meant to hurt you, Bro. You just don't know how sorry I am." Now tears were streaming down Shawn's face, too.

Isaiah grabbed him in a hug. "I can't keep letting this come between us. I love you, Shawn."

"I love you too, Isaiah. Please, please forgive me," he begged.

Isaiah released him and stepped back, wiping the tears from his face. "You are forgiven, Little Brother. I'll see you next weekend at the birthday party." With that, Isaiah opened the front door and headed for the cab waiting in the driveway.

Shawn went out on the porch to wave good-bye. He stayed out there until the cab had turned out of his long driveway. Coming back into the house, he closed the door and leaned against it. His brother had forgiven him. Just the thought of what had occurred in his foyer moments ago brought fresh tears to his eyes.

"That was beautiful."

Shawn quickly wiped his eyes and turned to see Lily leaning against the wall. In a teasing tone, he said, "If I'd known you'd be lurking around, sticking your nose in my business, I wouldn't have asked you to stay."

Lily smiled back. "Oh, you didn't just ask us to stay; you practically blackmailed me. But if you don't want us here, the boys and I can make our way home."

Shawn grabbed his crutch and made his way over to her. "Oh no, Baby. A deal is a deal. You're stuck with me for three days."

"I may have agreed to stay, but I didn't agree to do all the work." She lifted a baby bottle in the air. "Imani is ready to eat. So, Big Daddy, it's time for you to get acquainted with your daughter."

Back in the family room, Shawn sat down on the couch, and Lily put his little girl in his arms. "Wow," Shawn said. "It's been so long since the boys were this small, I didn't remember what a three-month-old baby felt like." Imani was so cuddly that Shawn couldn't resist bringing her up to his chest and wrapping his arms around her. It was at that moment that he realized he hadn't just wronged Lily, Shawnee, and Isaiah; in these last few months, he had been wronging his daughter every day of her young life. He turned to Lily. "I wish you were her mother."

Lily didn't respond. She just handed him the bottle, then sat down on the far side of the sectional.

As he fed Imani, he continued speaking his heart to Lily. "I have no right to ask you to be a part of our lives, because I know I messed up—"

"Yeah, you messed up all right, Buster." Lily cut into Shawn's tender moment.

She wasn't going to make this easy, but he wasn't about to give up. "Look, Lily. You and I weren't even together when I went out with Paris. You walked out on me, remember?"

"Oh, I remember. Do you remember the woman who claimed that you fathered her child?"

"And I told you when the court papers came that I didn't know the woman. You wouldn't listen and left me. When it was all said and done, the woman turned out to be some loon who had only dreamed about being with me."

"That woman may have been crazy, but you had to take a paternity test when we first got together. Do you remember that?"

Imani was going to town on that bottle of formula. Shawn watched her jaw work for a moment. "You and I had just gotten serious when my ex-girlfriend claimed I was the father of her baby. I told you about the situation, and you said you would stick by me."

"I was already pregnant. What did you expect me to do?"

Imani was sucking air. Lily got up and took the bottle away from Shawn. "You can't let her do that."

"Oh. Sorry about that, Imani-girl. Daddy will get the hang of all this soon enough." He needed to. Because, given Lily's anger, he couldn't promise his daughter that she would be getting a new mommy anytime soon. He lifted Imani onto his chest and began patting her back to burp her. "I always thought you stayed because you loved me, Lily. I mean, if it wasn't about love, then what was it about? The money?"

She looked ready to let him have it, when Shawnee and little Isaiah came barreling into the room, one pushing a toy Jeep, the other a Hummer.

⌒

Lily watched her children having the time of their lives, playing with toys that cost more than her monthly mortgage. And she had to admit, if only to herself, that Shawn's wealth had played a part in how long she had stayed with him. "I'm going to the kitchen to make dinner," she said, then walked out of the family room.

In the kitchen, Lily was reminded yet again of the difference between the haves and the have-nots. From the granite countertops to the handcrafted cherry cabinets, every detail spoke of Shawn's wealth. Lily had grown up on food stamps and government cheese. Her mother had worked two jobs in order to provide for the four children her alcoholic husband had abandoned when he'd left her for one of his coworkers.

A devout Christian, Lily's mother would pray continually about their situation and always told her children that God was going to turn things around. But Lily hadn't been interested in the slow turnaround her mother had been prepared to wait on. So, growing up, as men had started taking an interest in her, Lily had sworn that she would never fall in love with a man who wasn't financially secure.

She broke off her musings to concentrate on her dinner preparations. It seemed taco salad was on the menu tonight—something quick and easy. She opened a cabinet and pulled out a packet of taco seasoning. Before closing the cabinet door, she looked around and noticed that the shelves were full to bursting with canned goods and bags of rice and beans of numerous types.

When Lily had been a kid, the thing she'd hated most was beans. She'd determined that she would never eat any of those nasty beans her mother was always fixing. But one day, hunger pangs had ripped through her body, sending her to the kitchen in search of something—anything—to eat. The cabinets had been bare. She couldn't simply take a pack of meat out of the fridge, because there hadn't been any food there, either. The only thing to eat in the house that day had been a pot of red beans that her mother had fixed. Feeling as if she would die if she didn't put something in her stomach, Lily had grabbed a bowl and scooped some of those beans into it. She'd sat down at the kitchen table, taking a huge gulp, trying to convince herself that red beans wouldn't kill her.

She'd dipped her spoon into the concoction and brought it to her mouth. Her stomach had moaned from hunger, so she'd opened her mouth and swallowed the dread beans. But once her tongue had gotten a taste, Lily had realized that she liked beans. She'd gone on to eat the entire bowl, even returning to the stove for a second and then a third helping. When her mother had come inside, she'd found Lily holding the pot upside down, draining the juice out of it.

Her mother had laughed and told everybody she could, "The girl who doesn't eat beans now not only eats beans but will clean the pot afterward." She'd found the whole situation extremely funny. But, for Lily, the incident had set her find-a-rich-man plan in motion. By the time she turned sixteen, Lily flat out refused to date any guy who didn't have a job and a plan for getting out of the low-income neighborhood they lived in.

When none of the neighborhood guys had been found to measure up, Lily had begun looking for men in other circles. She'd met Shawn at a party attended by a lot of groupies and well-connected women hoping to land a rich guy. Shawn Morrison had everything Lily had been looking for: He was handsome, famous, and rich. To guarantee that she would never go hungry again, Lily would have married him in a heartbeat. The only problem with her plan was that she had fallen in love with Shawn, and he had broken her heart over and over again.

Funny thing was, now she would gladly take a poor man, if only he would promise not to break her heart.

Seven

Sunday morning—Lily's second day at Shawn's house, helping him with Imani while he rested his knee—she got up and went to church, just as if it were any other Sunday. God was her Source, and Lily would never lose sight of that fact again.

After leaving Shawn and then giving her life to Christ, Lily had struggled with the fear of being poor and having to pray for food to feed her children, just as her mother had done so many times after Lily's father had left them with nothing. But God had lovingly shown her His promises in the Scriptures. One of her favorites was Psalm 37:25: *"I have been young, and now am old; yet have I not seen the righteous forsaken, nor his seed begging bread."*

That Scripture, along with so many others, had given Lily hope. And now, as she sat in church, listening to the pastor preach from Psalm 49, Lily was reminded about something else: She was no longer fearful about living in poverty, for she had found her Source of joy. She finally understood how her mother had been able to look at the bare cabinets and empty refrigerator, bow down to the Lord and pray for food, and then get up with a smile on her face. Money wasn't the answer—it was trusting in God that brought true hope and joy to people.

To be honest, the only time Lily had gone hungry as a child had been the day she'd refused to eat the beans her mother had made. On day two, when her hunger pangs had hit and she'd dropped her pride, her belly had been full and satisfied. So, while her family may not have had everything they wanted, God had made sure that all their needs were met—and that was enough.

After leaving church, Lily rushed back to Shawn's house. She would be heading back home tomorrow night, so there was no time to waste. She was determined to help him see the truth—to make him understand why she no longer trusted in his riches but in God.

Shawn was in the family room with his leg propped up on the coffee table, watching the boys play with the train set he'd purchased for them last Christmas. Lily rushed into the room, her Bible under her arm.

"Good morning," Shawn greeted her as she sat down next to him. "I didn't get a chance to thank you for breakfast. Or dinner, for that matter. You made the best taco salad I've ever had and then scurried off before I had a chance to wipe my mouth and say thanks."

Lily shrugged. "I wasn't in the mood for company last night."

"Are you in the mood for company this morning?"

"Yes, but first, I want to talk to you about something…show you something, actually." She handed him her Bible. "Would you please read Psalm Forty-six, verses one through nine?"

Shawn hesitated before accepting the Bible. "What's this about?"

"I want to admit something to you." Shame for the girl she once was rose up within her for a moment, but then she allowed the blood that Jesus shed for her to wash it away. "Last night, when you asked me if I had stayed with you because of the money, I got offended."

"I never should have said something like that to you, Lily. I know you're not that kind of woman."

"But you were right, Shawn. I put up with a lot of the things you did to me because I was afraid of being poor. I grew up in poverty and didn't want to live that way as an adult." She looked over at her sons' smiling faces as they laughed and played with toys, the likes of which she had only dreamed of as a kid. She was thankful that they were on the other side of the family room and couldn't hear her conversation with Shawn. Even so, she lowered her voice before her next confession. "I lied to you about being on birth control when we first got together. That's why I ended up pregnant with Shawnee only three months into our relationship."

Shawn leaned back as if the wind had just been knocked out of him. "So, you never loved me? I thought you were different from Paris, but I was just a payday to you too, huh?"

She shook her head. "That's not true, Shawn. I don't deny that I was over the moon because you were interested in me and you were rich, but I did fall in love with you. I wanted to be with you more than anything. But you broke my heart over and over again. And that's when I realized that looks and wealth just weren't enough." She paused. "If you'll read the Scripture I asked you to, you'll begin to see what I'm talking about."

Shawn turned away, anger and disappointment etched across his face. He lowered his head and began reading aloud from Psalm 49.

> Hear this, all ye people; give ear, all ye inhabitants of the world: both low and high, rich and poor, together. My mouth shall speak of wisdom; and the meditation of my heart shall be of understanding. I will incline mine ear to a parable: I will open my dark saying upon the harp. Wherefore should I fear in the days of evil, when the iniquity of my heels shall compass me about? They that trust in their wealth, and boast themselves in the multitude of their riches; none of them can by any means redeem his brother, nor give to God a ransom for him: (for the redemption of their soul is precious, and it ceaseth for ever:) that he should still live for ever, and not see corruption.

Once Shawn finished reading, he looked up at Lily with questioning eyes.

"The day I decided to leave you, my mother had asked me to read those verses. In that moment, I finally faced the fact that you had not proven yourself worthy of all the trust I had placed in you."

"Don't you mean, all the trust you had placed in my money?"

She didn't deny his charge but rather trod on. "I came to understand that only God was worthy of all my trust, because He is the only One who can redeem us from our sins."

Shawn rolled his eyes.

"You don't believe me? Then tell me, Shawn, with all your greatness, how come you have never been able to mend the relationship with your brother until yesterday?"

"Because he wouldn't listen to me before."

"No, it was because it took God to redeem you back to Isaiah. I stood back and watched what happened between the two of you. When those tears started flowing down Isaiah's face, it wasn't simply because you were standing there with your same old goofy apology."

"Okay, if you know so much, then why was my brother crying like that?"

"Because God had finally moved on his heart, and Isaiah couldn't hold you hostage to his unforgiveness any longer. So, you need to be thanking God for redeeming you to your brother."

"And should I also thank God that the only woman I have ever wanted to spend my life with has just confessed to me that she was after my money?"

"Yes, because your money no longer impresses me. And, for some reason that only God knows, I love you still." After saying that, Lily took her Bible from Shawn and stood up. "I'm going to check on Imani. I'll be back down to fix you and the boys some lunch in a little while."

⌣

Until two years ago, Shawn never would have imagined that a woman could rip his heart out in such a fashion as Lily did on a regular basis. But what she had done to him this morning had been the worst. Shawn had always felt inferior to every other member of his family. He'd never been the smartest; that title had gone to Eric. He'd never been the kindest; that title had gone to Elaine, his youngest sister. Never the most talented; that had been Dee Dee, the superstar actress. He'd also never been the most handsome; that had been Isaiah, the heartthrob turned preacher.

But the one thing that he'd been proud of since the day he'd first met Lily was that he'd believed she loved him for who he was. Now he was learning that her love had come about because of what he had. Deep down, he had always harbored some lingering doubt. Hadn't that been the real reason he hadn't wanted to give his inheritance away? Because he thought he needed the money in order to impress others?

He stood up from the couch. "You boys stay in here and play," he told Shawnee and Isaiah. "I need to take care of something, and then I'll be back."

The nursery was upstairs. To reach it, Shawn had to walk with his crutch to the base of the spiral staircase, then hop up each step. But the pain his knee suffered was nothing compared to the pain Lily had inflicted on his heart, and he was about to have it out with her, right now.

He swung the door to the nursery open and then stood there for a moment, trying to recover from his arduous journey. Lily was in the rocking chair, holding Imani. She looked beautiful to him. So full of love and innocence—the way she'd looked while nursing his sons in that same chair. But she wasn't innocent.

"What are you doing up here, Shawn? You're sweating...are you in pain?" She got up from the chair and put the baby back in the crib. "Sit down. Let me go get you some pain pills."

Shawn lowered himself into the recliner beside the crib, thankful that Lily knew what to do. When she'd lived with him, she'd become an expert on which painkillers to give him and when, depending on whether they were sleep-inducing or not. It wasn't that Shawn enjoyed popping pills; but being topped by three-hundred-pound guys, game after game, his body needed help healing itself.

"Here." Lily handed him some Motrin caplets and a glass of water. This would do the trick.

After he'd swallowed the medicine, Lily reached out her hands. "Lean on me. Let's get you to your bed so you can lie down. I want to have a look at your knee."

He wanted to protest, but he was in so much pain from that little hop-the-stairs stunt that he couldn't even figure out how to form an argument. He stood, then leaned on Lily's shoulder and let her help him to his bed. When he was lying down, she pushed up the cuff of his pants and began examining his knee like a pro. Shawn tucked his hands under his head and leaned back against the pillows, letting Lily tend to him as she had done so often after previous injuries.

"It's swollen. Let me grab the massage oil from your bathroom."

"Can't let your cash cow stay on the injured list for too long, can you?"

Lily left the room without responding. She returned moments later. "Let me know if I'm hurting you," she said as she began massaging his leg.

He closed his eyes, trying to block out the feel of her touch. She was hurting him, all right, but not by anything she was doing to his leg. "You know, Lily, right now, I'm wondering if you truly understood those Scriptures that you asked me to read."

"I understood them."

"Oh, really? Then, why haven't you ever asked me to forgive you? Because, right now, it seems to me that you're the one in need of redemption."

"What?" Her hands froze for a moment. "Has your pain medicine kicked in already? Because you have started talking crazy if you think I need to apologize to you."

She resumed working magic on his leg, causing him to feel things he didn't want to feel at the moment. He pushed her hand away and sat up. "You used me, and you don't think you owe me an apology?"

Lily sat down on the edge of the bed. "You cheated on me with every groupie you could find. I think I've paid enough for my sins against you."

"Do you really? Well, let me enlighten you, Ms. Lily Washington. You never believed anything I said to you—you never listened at all. I've already admitted that I was dating other women when we first met. But after you told me that you were pregnant with Shawnee…." He waved a hand in the air. "I don't even care that you tricked me, because Shawnee and little Isaiah are the best. I'm glad they're my sons. But I stopped seeing those other women for you, and you never appreciated that fact. All you did was constantly accuse me of sleeping around, when it wasn't even true."

"How can you say it wasn't true, Shawn? Women were always calling you, and then there were those paternity tests you had to take."

"I can't stop people from calling my phone. But, if you'll remember, I had my house number changed when you moved in. But even that wasn't good enough for you. You made me feel like dirt because women wanted to falsely accuse me of being their baby's daddy, when, all the while, you were just using me as a cash register."

Lily put up her hand. "Okay, maybe you have a point. Maybe I am—or was—a big hypocrite. But it hurts to feel like I wasn't enough for you."

"And it hurts to feel like an ATM machine," Shawn shot back.

"Point taken. And believe me, I have learned my lesson." She stood up. "I need to go check on the boys."

She got as far as the door when he said, "You didn't find me even a little bit handsome when we first met?"

Lily whirled around. She looked at Shawn for a moment. "Baby, don't sell yourself short. I might have been grateful that you were rich, but it's always been about you." She took her time looking him over. "I was mesmerized by those deep dimples, those big brown eyes and bushy eyebrows...not to mention the fact that you're all chiseled and buff. I don't even know why I'm telling you all this. You're gorgeous, and you know it. I'm just giving you a fatter head than you already have." She turned and left the room without another word.

Eight

Shawn sat in the kitchen with Lily, ready to talk with Melvin Cotrell and Detective Jones. The kids were asleep, so they were able to speak freely about Paris Holmes. Detective Jones had pen and paper in hand, and Melvin nodded toward Shawn.

"Okay," he began. "First off, Detective Jones, I want you to know that I will do everything I can to help you find Paris's killer."

Jones raised his eyebrows. "I wish you had felt this way a few days ago. The trail is getting colder by the minute."

"I know, and I'm sorry about that. But I couldn't tell you why I went over to Paris's house until I made sure I wouldn't hurt Lily in doing so."

"Why would Ms. Washington be affected by what you had to tell me?" Jones asked.

"Shawn went to see Paris because I asked him to talk to her," Lily supplied.

"I see." Jones nodded. "And why did you ask him to talk to her?"

"Paris had been bothering me ever since Imani was born. First, she wanted me to talk to Shawn and get him to admit that Imani was his, but I couldn't do that. So then, she got this harebrained idea about us being on a reality show together."

"What kind of reality show?" Jones asked.

"Something about football wives…but I told her that I wasn't married to Shawn, so I wasn't going on any show with such a title.

Nor would I do any reality show, for that matter. The women on those shows are too catty."

"Okay, you mentioned that Paris Holmes wanted you to convince Shawn to claim his daughter, but you didn't want to. Why is that?"

"I can answer that question for you, Detective," Shawn piped up. "If I claimed Imani as my child, Lily was worried that she might end up getting less child support money each month."

Lily hit him in the arm. "Stop being a jerk."

"Stop being a gold digger."

"You know what? I wish I'd never said anything to you at all. You are so childish." Lily stood up and stalked out of the room without a backward glance.

Jones frowned at Shawn. "Did you really have to antagonize her during the interview?"

"I wasn't trying to antagonize anybody," Shawn protested. "I was just stating a fact."

"Well, all right then, Mr. Fact-Stater, is the money issue the reason you thought Ms. Washington might have killed Paris Holmes?"

Shawn raised his hands, calling for a time-out. "Whoa, wait a minute. I never said I thought Lily killed anybody." He pointed in the direction Lily had gone when she'd stormed out. "Go ask her. The night Paris was killed, Lily was at church with about seven hundred witnesses."

"Fine. Since the two of you obviously can't be in the same room together, I'll finish with you first and then go ask her." Jones made a note on his pad. "So, why did Lily ask you to speak with Paris?"

Shawn was hesitant to answer. He was worried that in his anger, he might say something that would hurt Lily. And no matter how ticked off he was with her, he would never want to cause her harm.

Melvin must have sensed his anxiety. "Shawn, we've already gone over this. Lily will be fine. You need to cooperate with Detective Jones."

"All right, all right." Shawn looked at Detective Jones. "Here's the thing. Paris called up Lily to gloat when the DNA test results came back. She told Lily that she didn't need her for that reality show anymore because she had Imani."

"So, Ms. Washington was jealous?" Jones asked.

"Yeah. At least, I assumed she was jealous, but now I don't know."

"Of course I was jealous, you idiot!"

All three men turned to the doorway where Lily stood, glaring at Shawn.

She looked at Detective Jones. "I came back because I remembered something that might be of use."

"Come back and sit down with us," Jones suggested.

Lily glared at Shawn again before addressing Jones once more. "That's all right; it won't take long. The last time I spoke with Paris, she told me that I could have Shawn, because she no longer wanted him. Evidently she had a new man."

"I see. And did she tell you who this new man was?"

"Not in so many words. But I got the impression that it was the man who she claimed was going to produce that crazy reality show."

Detective Jones scribbled something on his notepad. "Did you get this producer's name?"

Lily's brow furrowed. "It was Jason something. Yeah, his first name is Jason. I don't remember his last name, but I bet one of the wives would know."

"What wives?" Jones asked. "Who are you talking about?"

"Paris set up a meeting about a month ago with several of the football players' wives in order to get the ball rolling on that reality show."

"Okay, I'll try to track them down," Jones said. "I think I have a handle on what happened between you all and Paris that day, but, Ms. Washington, can you tell me where you were last Wednesday?"

"During the day and evening?" Lily asked.

"Around eight at night."

"I was at church. We have Wednesday night Bible study, and I always attend."

"What's the name of your church?" Jones asked, pen poised.

"Tabernacle of Faith. It's in the Fifth Ward."

"Thanks. I'll be in touch again if I have any more questions." Jones and Melvin stood and prepared to make their exit. "Will you be staying here for a while, Ms. Washington?"

"No, I'm going home tonight, but you can reach me at the number I gave you."

"Well, thanks again for the help," Jones said, then disappeared into the hallway.

Lily followed him. "Not a problem," Shawn heard her say. "Even though Paris and I had our differences, I truly hope you find her killer."

"It was good of you to want to help," he heard Melvin tell her. "Most people in your shoes would have just stayed out of it."

"Thank you for being here to help Shawn, Mr. Cotrell," Lily said.

When the door shut behind the two men, Shawn entered the foyer. "What's this about you leaving tonight? You owe me another night, remember?"

Lily spun around, looking ready to do battle. "If you think I'm staying in this house with you another ten minutes, you need to think again. I'm going to collect my boys and get out of here."

"Oh, so you're just going to renege on a promise like that, huh? I thought keeping your word meant something to you Christians."

She seemed to calm a bit at those words.

He started walking toward her.

"I do strive to keep my promises," she said, "but I don't like having my words twisted and turned around into something other than what I said."

He was in front of her now, so close that he could feel the warmth of her breath as she exhaled. "So, when you admitted that you wanted to date me because I had money, I shouldn't have taken that to mean that you were a gold digger?"

"Yes. I mean, no. Look, you're making things out to be worse than they really are."

He stepped up to her, pinning her against the wall with his chest. "Then explain it to me, Lily. Because I really need to know what was real between us and what wasn't."

"It was all real, Shawn. I don't know what you want me to say."

He rubbed her cheek with the back of his hand. "When I touch you, how does it feel?"

She was shivering. "I like it when you touch my face."

He bent down and nibbled her neck. "You used to go wild when I kissed your neck like this. Did you really like that, or were you just pretending?"

She closed her eyes and moaned, giving him all the answer he needed.

Shawn touched his lips to Lily's and kissed her like a starving man who'd been given a plate of food. Their bodies melded together as Lily wrapped her arms around him and feasted upon his lips, as well. When they came up for air, Shawn held her and rested his chin on top of her head. With a husky voice, he asked, "When I kiss you like that, are you kissing me back because you want me, or my paycheck?"

❦

Lily pushed Shawn away. She had temporally lost her mind when he'd started touching her, but that paycheck remark had brought her back to reality quick, fast, and in a foot-stomping hurry. "Get away from me."

She ran upstairs, woke up her kids, and told them to go give their father a kiss good-bye.

Shawnee was the first to protest. "I want to stay here, Mommy."

"Well, you can't. Now go do what I said so we can go."

Shawnee and little Isaiah made their way down the stairs. Shawn was waiting at the bottom. They hugged him, and then little Isaiah said, "Come with us, Daddy."

Lily came down the stairs with purse and keys in hand. "Daddy needs to stay here with baby Imani, Honey."

"Why can't baby Imani come with us?" Shawnee asked, starting to cry. "Why can't we all just stay here?"

"Don't cry, Son. I'm sorry about all this. But I'll make it up to you, okay?" Shawn promised.

As they walked out the door, Lily was wondering who in the world was going to make this up to her. How many times could she fall for the same creep in one lifespan?

Nine

As usual, instead of dealing with the issues he was having with Lily, Shawn tried to hook up with another woman. He had promised Jules Moore that he was going to take her out to help her get over the breakup with her ex-boyfriend. Secretly, though, he was hoping that Jules could help him get over Lily.

"So, what do you want to do today?" Jules asked as she lounged with Shawn on the sectional in his family room.

"You know my knee is all busted up, girl. What more do you want me to do besides prop this leg up and look at your beautiful self?"

She moved closer to Shawn and blew in his ear. "I thought that since you called, you wanted to go out or something." There was an emphasis on the something.

Oh yeah, Shawn wanted to do *something* with Jules, all right. But he had been tricked by Paris and Lily, and he wasn't trying for his third strike. "I need to let my knee heal," was his excuse. "Got to get back on the field and earn my paycheck."

"You've been on the injured list a lot this past year. What's up with that?"

Shawn hated when people asked about his injured status. It made him feel like a loser, because after signing a twenty-million-dollar contract, he had lost his focus. The fight wasn't in him anymore, and he was losing his love for the game. At twenty-nine,

Shawn was hoping to hang in there just two more years so that he could fulfill his contract and then retire. He picked up the TV remote and started flipping through the channels. "You wanna watch a movie?"

"Whatever." Jules leaned back against the couch again. "I'm just glad you want to spend time with me."

He really didn't want to spend time with Jules, or any other woman who wasn't Lily. But he had burned that bridge. He'd also hired a nanny to help him with Imani, so he'd had a lot of time on his hands this past week. Maybe one day, he would learn that trying to fill up his free time with indiscriminate women was not the answer. And maybe today was the day that he wouldn't just bring his books to school but actually open them up and learn something new.

When the movie was over, Jules turned to Shawn. "Thanks for inviting me over. I always knew that you and I could be good together. I just had to sit back and wait on you to get over your latest problem."

Shawn frowned. "The thing is, you weren't just sitting back waiting. You had a man, remember?"

A look of sorrow crossed Jules's lovely face. "But that didn't work out, did it? And now we're back together, so all's well that ends well, is what I say."

He couldn't let Jules believe that they were together, as in a couple. He put his head in his hand as he realized his mistake. Jules had always been clingy and quick to jump from one bed to the next. He looked back up at her, trying to figure out the best way to end this. He decided on the simple truth. "The thing is, Jules, I haven't really gotten over Lily yet. I still want her, but she doesn't want me. To be honest, I called you over here tonight to try to get her off my mind. But it's not working."

Her eyes filled with a kind of pain he'd never noticed there before. She stood up. "Don't call me again—not until you get her out of your system."

Once Jules was gone, Shawn checked his phone, wanting desperately to pick it up and call Lily to apologize. But everything in him called him ten different kinds of fools for even thinking about doing something like that. Lily had wronged him. She needed to beg his forgiveness, but instead, she was angry because he had the nerve to call it like he saw it.

But in some ways, Shawn also realized that the "gold digger" label didn't fit Lily. If she really wanted him for his money, why hadn't she married him, demanded a divorce, and earned herself a nice sum in alimony? And why hadn't she tried to get an increase in the child support payments that she'd been receiving for the past two years? Most of the athletes he knew who had children outside of wedlock complained constantly about the mother taking them back to court for cost-of-living increases. But Lily had never asked for anything like that. She lived in a modest home and saved a large portion of her child support payments for a college fund for Shawnee and little Isaiah.

Maybe he should apologize. He picked up his phone, preparing to call, when Martha, the nanny, walked into the room carrying Imani.

"I think this little one wants to spend some time with her daddy," Martha said.

Shawn put down his phone and let Martha place Imani in his arms. "She wouldn't stop crying, huh?"

"She'll get used to me. It usually takes a while."

It hadn't taken Imani any time at all to connect with Lily. As a matter of fact, he hardly remembered Imani crying much when Lily had her. Maybe his daughter knew a good thing when she saw it, too. Maybe it was just her dad who was a bit slow. Shawn looked down at Imani and started making cooing sounds. The baby smiled, and Shawn found himself grinning, as well. "What is Daddy going to do with you, pretty girl?"

"I'll go make her a bottle," Martha said, then left the room.

Shawn remembered that his father's birthday party was this weekend. He would be heading to Atlanta in two days. "I'm going to take you to a party and show you off to my entire family, that's what I'm going to do."

Joel Morrison was going to have a lot of questions for him. Shawn just hoped he was ready to provide answers.

That weekend, the gang was all there, and for the first time in two years, Shawn felt like a welcome member of the Morrison family. When he got out of the car at his father's ranch, the boys ran ahead of him into the house. He stood there remembering the feelings of estrangement he'd experienced so often since the revelation of his indiscretion. The rift between him and Isaiah had been one of the hardest things Shawn had ever endured. He hadn't wanted to be around his family once the truth had come out, because he'd felt so ashamed of what he had done.

But his father hadn't taken sides. Shawn remembered the talk they'd had on the steps of his father's beach house in the Bahamas as if it had happened yesterday.

Shawn cringed when his father approached him on the beach house steps. He just wanted to be alone.

His dad put his hand on Shawn's shoulder. "I don't have any rocks to throw at you."

Shawn relaxed a little. "I knew it was wrong when I was doing it. But I just kept telling myself that it was no big deal because Isaiah had only been dating Tanya about a month when I came home that summer."

Joel sat down next to Shawn and patted him on the leg. "I was young once, Son. I know how things can get out of hand. And while I never slept with my brother's girl, or even a close friend's girl, for that matter, I did my share of wrongs before giving my life to the Lord."

Shawn tilted his head toward the door, indicating his family inside the house. "They're all treating me like a leper or something."

Joel laughed and patted Shawn on the shoulder as he stood up. "There are no lepers in my family, Son. God has cleansed you from the inside out; you just haven't taken off your dirty clothes yet." With that, Joel walked into the house, humming as if all of his children's dirty secrets hadn't just been laid out at the dinner table.

As Shawn thought back to that moment, he realized that his father truly didn't have a care in the world. Joel Morrison looked at his children through the eyes of God and saw what was to be, not what was or is.

Feeling a surge of enthusiasm, Shawn put Imani in her stroller, then strode into the house and burst into the ballroom. "Let's get this party started!"

Elaine ran over and hugged him. "Why do you always have to be late?"

"Yeah," Dee Dee agreed. "I'm supposed to be the only diva in this family. You should at least arrive before me."

Shawn laughed. "I'll keep that in mind from now on. But I'm traveling with my kids this weekend, and they tend to slow me down."

Elaine looked over Shawn's shoulder at the stroller where Imani lay. "I was sorry to hear about your daughter's mother, Shawn."

"I was out of the country, or I would have rushed to your side," Dee Dee explained.

"Don't worry about it. Isaiah came and helped me out; I'm good."

"Can I hold the baby?" Elaine asked.

Shawn stepped aside. "Of course. I need to go find Shawnee and little Isaiah. They took off the moment we got out of the car."

"I saw them in the movie room with Dad and Isaiah," Dee Dee said.

"What are they doing in there?" Shawn asked.

"Dad is having a video conference with Eric and Linda. Linda's still on bed rest, you know, so they can't travel, but they wanted to wish Dad a happy birthday."

Shawn made his way to the theater. He stood outside the door, watching his sons jump up and down with their cousin, Erin, waving and shouting their greetings at Eric, Linda, and Kivonna.

"We wish you guys were here," Erin said in her sweet little princess voice.

"Me too, but we're stuck in this boring old house," Kivonna complained.

"On that note, I guess we'll let you get back to your party, Dad," Eric said. "And remember, we'll all come to see you as soon as the baby gets here." He had his arms around his wife and daughter, and he looked like the happiest man on earth.

Shawn wished his family was complete and that he could look that happy, even in the face of adversity. Eric had just lost an election, and his wife's pregnancy was high-risk, with lots of uncertainty. Yet even Linda appeared to be at peace as she waved and said, "We'll see you soon, Daddy."

"Love you, Linda-girl," Joel said. "You take care of that new grandbaby of mine."

"Will do," Eric answered, and then the screen went blank.

"Call 'em back, Pop-Pop!" Little Isaiah grabbed his grandfather's arm.

"Not now, Little Man. We need to go back to the ballroom." Joel stood up and turned to the door. His eyes lit up when he saw Shawn. "I knew you had to be roaming around here somewhere when I saw these two munchkins."

"We're not munchkins, Pop-Pop," Shawnee insisted. "We're young men."

Joel laughed. "That you are." He patted his grandson's shoulder. "Come on, everybody; let's get back to the party."

As the group filed out of the room, Joel stopped and gave Shawn a hug. "I'm glad you came to see your old man."

"You know I wouldn't miss your big day, Dad." Shawn's eyes turned to Isaiah. There was an awkward pause, but then Shawn remembered what Lily had said about God redeeming him to his brother. He walked over to Isaiah and gave him a bear hug. "Thanks for your help last week."

Isaiah gave him a playful shove. "Boy, you know I'd go to the ends of the earth to come see about you."

"I know it now," Shawn said, grateful he could mean what he said. He knew that he could never deserve his brother's forgiveness, but he was standing there, hungrily receiving it anyway.

When their father had left the room, Isaiah lowered his voice and said, "I just talked to Melvin a little while ago. He says that the information you and Lily gave the police has helped them narrow down a suspect."

"That's great," said Shawn. "I'll give him a call after the party."

The celebration went on for hours. Around midnight, Shawn could tell that his father was getting tired, so he asked him, "Do you want to go bed?"

"I think I should," Joel agreed. "Walk me to my room, Son."

Shawn did as he was told. In the bedroom, he helped his father into bed and pulled the covers up for him. "Do you need anything else?" Shawn asked with concern. At that moment, his father looked every bit as old as his eighty-five years.

"I just want to talk to you for a minute. Is that all right?"

Shawn wanted to say no, because he knew this wasn't going to be a "How's life been treating you?" kind of talk. It was a "Come to Jesus" talk, and Shawn didn't know if he had the energy to resist anymore. He sat down on the edge of the bed. "What's up?"

"Why haven't you been to see my accountant about setting up your foundation?"

"Wow, no beating around the bush; you just get straight down to business, huh, Dad?"

"At my age, I don't have time to beat around the bush."

"Dad, I gave you back that charity money, remember?"

Joel took Shawn's hand and gripped it tightly. "You know that I lost my first wife and our three children on the same day, years before you were born."

Shawn nodded. He knew the story, although his father rarely talked about it. When they were kids, Joel would read to them from every book of the Bible but one: the book of Job. No one noticed, until Isaiah, as a Bible-toting teenager, had gathered the siblings together and told them what he'd read in the book their father had avoided. "This account sounds just like what Dad went through," Isaiah had told them. "He's a modern-day Job."

Shawn hadn't thought much of it through the years, but now that he had children of his own, he knew for sure that if what had happened to his dad were to happen to him, Shawn would probably curse God and then blow his brains out. But not Joel Morrison. His father amazed him.

"My children were lost to me in a matter of minutes. I couldn't help them, because I was on location shooting a film when they burned in the fire. But I'm here for you, Son."

"You've always been here for me, Dad. I just don't understand why I need to give away money that should rightfully come to me as my inheritance."

"My first three children never received any monetary inheritance from me. But do you know what they received from me?"

Shawn shook his head.

"Every day of my children's lives, I gave them Jesus. I helped them understand how important it is to love and serve God, and for that reason, I believe that I will see those three children again in heaven."

"You taught us about God while we were growing up, too," Shawn said, "and I remember a verse in the Bible that said something like, 'A man who doesn't provide for his family is worse than an infidel.' I still haven't figured out what an infidel is, but I'm sure you don't want to be worse than it."

"Let me finish, Shawn. Yes, money is nice to have. I don't deny that I have enjoyed being able to do whatever I want, whenever I want. But God blessed me with more money than I or my children could spend in a lifetime, and neither you nor I can take it with us when this life is over. So now, let me ask you two simple questions that come straight out of the Bible: *'What shall it profit a man, if he shall gain the whole world, and lose his own soul? Or what shall a man give in exchange for his soul?'*"

Shawn didn't have an answer for his father.

Joel continued on. "The blessing is in the giving, Son. I mean, you've made a good living for yourself. Don't you have enough?"

"See, that's what I mean." Shawn stood and began pacing the room. It was easier, now that his knee was feeling better. "Everybody thinks I have so much money and tons more on the way. But I don't think anyone's paying attention to how many times I've been on the injured list this year and last. My back hurts like I don't know what. I'll need surgery on my knee in another year or so. My career is trending down. Meaning my money-making years are almost over."

"That's not true, Shawn. Even if you aren't playing football, you've made such a name for yourself that you'll be making money off of endorsements for years to come. The sky is the limit for you and for all of the Morrison children. Don't you see that?"

Shawn sat back down. "Do you really think I can have a career outside of football?"

"Of course I do. Son, I have prayed for all of my children over the years, but I've prayed for you the most—because, for some reason, you don't seem to realize just how special you are."

Shawn closed his eyes and inhaled, as if to breathe in his father's words. He needed to hear this, especially now. He hadn't wanted to donate that money because it felt like giving his future away, but maybe his father was right. Maybe he would be able to handle his future all by himself. It was time for him to stop being selfish and start joining his family in giving away their wealth. "All right, Dad. I'll do it."

"Thank you, Son. And remember, you can't beat God at giving. You do this, and all you'll have to do is stand back and wait for His blessings to overtake you."

The party finally ended, and, after putting the kids to bed, Shawn kicked off his shoes, stretched across his own bed, and checked his phone for missed calls. There were two from Lily, and one from Melvin Cotrell. He knew he should call Melvin first. Lily was only calling to find out how the boys were doing—he could give her that information after he talked to Melvin. But his fingers hit the call button on Lily's number instead of Melvin's. He leaned back against the pillows and waited for her to answer.

"Hey Shawn, how's it going?"

"It's going. The boys are asleep, though."

"At midnight, your time, I would hope that you had put them to bed hours ago."

"I barely managed. Those little monsters refused to sleep unless I gave them another slice of chocolate cake."

Lily laughed. "Those kids eat too many sweets. I wonder if I can pray away cavities."

"They'll be fine. I'm the one you need to be praying for."

"Why you? What's wrong?" He could hear the concern in her voice.

"I think I just lost my mind."

"What do you mean?"

"I might actually be crazy. I'm serious, Lily. I just had a talk with my father and let him convince me to give away a hundred million dollars."

Lily let out an excited scream. "You haven't lost your mind at all. You're doing a wonderful thing. I'm so proud of you, Shawn."

"I'm surprised that you're happy about this."

"I don't know why my happiness should surprise you."

"Well, let's see...if I had been able to keep my inheritance instead of give it away, your monthly child support payments would have increased, for one."

Lily laughed again, but this time Shawn got the distinct impression that she was laughing at him.

"I don't need your money, Shawn. What you give me to take care of the boys is more than enough. Anything that we lack, I just trust and believe that God will make a way for us. You don't seem to understand that I know what it's like to be poor and not know where my next meal or a new pair of shoes will be coming from. Our kitchen cupboards were almost always bare, and my mother had to trust God every day to help her feed a house full of hungry mouths. I truly admire your father for teaching his children how to bless others who are in need."

Her words took him aback. "I guess I never looked at your life like that before. I knew that your mother didn't live in the nicest of neighborhoods, but I never even wondered what it was like for you growing up there."

"That's because you've always been rich, Shawn."

Shawn knew that what Lily was saying was the truth. All this time, he had been so busy focusing on his insecurities within his family that he'd never stopped to think just how blessed he was to have been born into a family such as the Morrisons.

Well, he might be slow to the game, but he would soon be scoring some Super-Bowl-worthy touchdowns. "A few years back, me and a couple of teammates helped out at a food pantry. I think I'll make that one of my top priorities when I get my foundation up and running."

"Yeah, since you've been accused of fathering so many babies, you might as well help single mothers feed their kids," Lily said with a giggle.

Shawn was being laughed at again, but he knew he deserved that one. "Lily?"

"Yeah?"

"If I could turn back time, I wouldn't have dated Paris. I would have waited for you to discover the truth about that woman who falsely accused me of being her child's father…I would have just waited until you came back to me."

"I know that you wish things had worked out that way, but they didn't," Lily said simply.

"I wish you could forgive me."

"And I wish you could stop thinking that I'm after your money."

"I think I'm beginning to figure that out. So, the ball's back in your court."

"Whatever," she said and then hung up the phone.

Shawn laid his cell phone down next to him on the bed and closed his eyes. He was only going to close his eyes for a few minutes and then get up and call Melvin, but he found himself drifting into a make-believe world where Lily loved him back…and he couldn't let the moment go. He stayed with his dream girl all night long, whispering sweet words of love into her ear.

She, in turn, showered him with expressions of love and adoration. Because, in his dream world, it didn't matter that Lily was a poor girl from a bad neighborhood and he was a rich boy who'd been given so much but appreciated so little. All that mattered was the love they had for each other. And in the morning when he woke up, Shawn was determined to do everything possible to turn his dreams into reality.

Ten

Shawn and the boys had breakfast with his family while Imani slept. After breakfast, his father's driver took them to the airport. It wasn't until they were waiting at the gate that Shawn remembered the missed call he'd received from Melvin Cotrell. He took out his phone and called his attorney.

On the third ring, Melvin answered. "Hey, I'm sorry I missed your call yesterday," Shawn told him. "Isaiah told me that the police have got some new evidence or something."

"They don't just have new evidence—they have a suspect. Her prints were found on Paris's brand-new Gucci bag, given to her by Jason Brooks just that morning."

Little Isaiah was playing with his Spider-Man toy. He got up and tried to walk off, slinging web as he went. Shawn grabbed him by the back of his shirt and sat him back down. "So, Lily was right about that producer's name being Jason?"

"She was so right that Detective Jones would like to give her a kiss."

"Tell him to keep his lips to himself," Shawn said, seeing red at the thought of another man coming near Lily.

"Anyway, Jason Brooks told Detective Jones that he'd just broken up with a woman who had threatened Paris, but he hadn't thought anything of it until Paris got stabbed."

"That's crazy. Paris steals this guy from some woman who goes ballistic and kills her?"

"Exactly. Evidently this Jules woman is bipolar and occasionally goes off her meds or something."

Shawn took the cell phone away from his ear and cleared the wax out with his fingertip. He must have heard wrong. He'd met only one woman named Jules the entire time he'd lived in New Orleans. Melvin couldn't have just said that name. "What's the name of the ex-girlfriend again?"

"Jules Moore…or something like that."

"What do you mean, 'or something like that'? Either her name is Jules Moore or it's not," Shawn yelled. Other travelers who had previously been minding their own business turned and stared at him. He ignored them.

"There's no reason to get hot under the collar," Melvin said. "Let me check my notes." There was a pause. "Yes, her name is Jules Moore."

The airline had begun boarding first-class passengers, so Shawn picked up the baby carrier and began escorting the boys toward the door. "Look, Melvin, my plane is about to take off. I need you to do me a favor."

"What's that?"

"Can you please call Detective Jones and ask him to go check on Lily? I think Jules might try to stir up some trouble with her."

"You know this woman?"

Shawn sighed. "Yes…we used to date, but I broke up with her when I started seeing Lily for the first time, years ago. She was just at my house the other night. Look, I've got to let you go. Please call Detective Jones." Shawn ended the call, handed over his ticket, and ushered his children onto the plane faster than he'd ever moved a piece of sheepskin down a football field.

Once he and the boys were buckled in their seats, he called Lily. The phone rang four times before switching over to voice mail. He hung up and dialed again. The phone went straight to voice mail this time. He looked at his watch. It was ten in the morning. Lily was probably at church, and she would have turned off her phone to avoid having it ring during the service. When the beep sounded, he decided to leave a message. "Lily, this is Shawn. Call me as soon as you get this message. No, scratch that. I'm on the plane getting ready to fly home. Call Detective Jones or my attorney ASAP; they'll tell you what's going on."

"Daddy, what's going on?" Shawnee asked. "Why you acting so nervous?"

"I'm not nervous, Son. Just sit back and chill."

First class had finished boarding, and other passengers were filing down the aisle. Soon Shawn would be forced to turn off his phone; he'd have no further connection to the outside world until he landed. He didn't know what to do. He wasn't positive that Jules would try something with Lily, but something in his gut told him she would. Especially when he remembered how uneasy he'd felt when Jules had called Lily his "problem."

Shawn didn't want to upset his father with the news, so he decided to call his big brother Isaiah—the same guy who'd been getting him out of scrapes since Shawn learned to walk; the same guy that he had wronged so deeply and had also been forgiven by. When Isaiah answered his phone, Shawn said, "Thank God you aren't already on the plane headed back home. I need your help."

Without hesitation, Isaiah asked, "What's up, Bro? How can I help?"

Shawn relayed the story about his breakup with Jules years ago so that he could be with Lily, and how he'd attempted to hook up with Jules again recently but then told her that he still preferred Lily. He then told Isaiah that the police suspected Jules as the person who'd killed Paris. "I need you to pray for Lily. It's going to take me a few hours to get to her."

"Of course I'll pray for Lily," Isaiah assured him. "I'll also pray for you and all these bonehead predicaments you keep getting yourself into."

Shawn was beside himself with grief for the harm his actions might bring to the woman he loved. "Please do pray for me, Bro. Lily and I need all the prayer we can get. Please ask God to help us. I swear, man, if He does, I'll never turn my back on Him again."

"From your mouth to God's ears, my brother." Isaiah started praying while they were still on the phone together, until a flight attendant approached Shawn and asked him to turn his cell phone off.

"I got to go, Isaiah, but keep praying."

"All right, man. Call me when you get home."

The flight attendant then handed him a couple of tissues. Shawn hadn't even realized he'd been crying.

"Thank you," he said, taking them and wiping his eyes.

"Not a problem," she said with a smile. She put her hand on Shawn's shoulder. "Keep the faith. God's got this one under control."

$\backsim$

"Pastor knows he stomped on the devil's head with that message this morning," Lily said to Gloria, a new friend from church, as they walked down the hall.

"He didn't just stomp on old Lucifer; he buried that bugaboo."

Lily laughed and gave her a playful slap on the back. "Girl, you silly."

"Don't you have to get your boys?" Gloria nodded at the children's church.

"No, the boys are with their father this weekend."

"So, what are you going to do with your kid-free day?"

"Well, since my mom is also out of town, I was thinking about some mall therapy. I'll probably grab myself a quick bite to eat and then head out."

"Sounds good, girl. If I had some extra cash, I'd go with you, but I'm saving every penny to pay to get my roof fixed."

"How old is your roof?"

"I bought the house ten years ago, and the roof was already about a decade old. I know that most people would just let the roof cave in and then call the insurance company, but my grandmother lives with me, and I would just die if she got hurt because I hadn't fixed the roof."

Since Lily lived in a modest home and didn't overspend in order to keep up appearances, she was not only able to save for her children's college funds, but she also had money set aside in a savings account for herself. And right now, shopping didn't seem like a priority. She put her hand on Gloria's arm, slowing her stride. "Gloria, can you sit down in the fellowship hall with me for a moment?"

"Sure, girl." They sat down at a table off to the side. "What's up?"

"I wanted to see if I could help you. How much have you saved for your roof, and how much more do you need?"

Gloria waved her off. "I am not taking your money, Lily."

"Can you just answer the question?"

Gloria leaned back in her seat and smiled at Lily. "My house is small, so the roof isn't that big. But the lowest estimate I received was for five thousand. I have about thirty-five hundred set aside right now, so I should have the rest in another year."

"In another year, the estimate will go up." Lily opened her purse and took out her checkbook. "Look, I don't need to go shopping. I was only going to do it to get my mind off of Shawn."

"What's he done now?" Gloria asked. "And don't you write that check. The quickest way for friends to become enemies is to loan each other money."

"Shawn has been trying to get back with me, and I'm just not sure if I can trust him with my heart like that." Lily paused. "I'm not loaning you anything. And you can't tell me who to give my money to. Don't you believe what your Bible says?"

"Of course I believe the Bible. I wouldn't call myself a Christian if I didn't."

"Well, my Bible says that it is more blessed to give than to receive. So, my giving this money to you will cause God to bless me in other ways, just like your opening up your home to your grandmother has caused Him to send me to help you with your roof. See how it works?" Smiling, Lily lowered her head, wrote out the check, tore it out, and handed it over.

Gloria sat there, looking dumbfounded.

"Go make your house safe for your granny."

Gloria stood up and hugged Lily as if she'd just been given a million dollars. "Girl, I don't know how to thank you for this. I mean, what can I do for you?"

"You still don't get it, do you?" Lily got to her feet, as well. "I believe that God will bless me for my kindness to you. I don't know what form His blessing will come in, but I do know that if you bless me back, He doesn't have to. So, don't you do anything for me. You got it?"

Gloria grinned. "Okay, I got it. Thank you." She hugged Lily again and then danced her way out the door.

As she watched her friend go, all Lily could think was that if giving away a measly fifteen hundred dollars made her feel this good, Shawn was about to be the happiest man on earth.

She had arrived at church late this morning, so she'd had to park on the street instead of in the parking lot. She crossed the street and got into her car. There would be no mall excursion for her today, but Lily wasn't the least bit saddened by that. Shawn might think of her as a gold digger, but she knew the truth. God had set her free from that mind-set and made her content with what she had.

She pulled into her driveway and got out of the car. As she was about to go up the steps to her front door, someone tapped her on the shoulder. Lily jumped, startled. She turned around and stared into the face of a beautiful woman with cold, hard eyes. She didn't know the woman's name, but she remembered her face—she used to date Shawn. She was one of the women he'd cheated on her with. "What do you want?" Lily asked. All the joy she'd been feeling had seeped out of her.

"I need to talk to you."

"I have no idea what this is about, and I really don't have time for drama." Lily turned away, but the woman grabbed her by the shoulder and held a knife under her chin.

"If you don't want to get stabbed in your driveway, I suggest you open the front door so we can go inside your house."

Eleven

"Why are you doing this?" Lily asked as she unlocked her front door.

"Just shut up and get inside." The woman shoved her into the house.

"I don't even know you, so I'm having trouble understanding why you would be upset with me."

"Women like you are all the same. You steal a girl's man without any concern for her or her feelings."

"What are you talking about? I don't know who your man is, but I can assure you that I didn't steal him. I'm not even dating anyone."

"Oh, you stole him, all right. You and those kids of yours got Shawn's head all turned around to the point where he doesn't want to have anything to do with me. He just dumped me. Like all he had to do was tell me that he was in love and wanted to be faithful, and I would just go away."

Lily was in shock. "Shawn said that to you?"

"Shut up. I'm tired of you and every woman in the world like you. Just sit down and shut up."

Lily sat down on her couch. She waited a few moments and then tried to reason with the woman. "Okay, you're right—I did make a move on Shawn, even though I knew he was seeing other women. But when I met him, he wasn't in a serious relationship, or

I never would have gotten with him. And besides, I don't understand why you would come at me about something that happened over seven years ago."

"You ask Shawn why I'm coming at you about this now." The woman touched the tip of her knife. "Oh, wait—you won't be seeing Shawn anymore, will you? Maybe I should tell you all about it right now, huh?"

~

Isaiah had appointed one of the elders at his church to preach the message this Sunday, so he wasn't scheduled to fly out of Atlanta until late afternoon. After getting the call from Shawn, he asked Ramona and Joel to pray with him. The three went into Joel's well-used prayer room and began bombarding heaven on behalf of Shawn and Lily.

~

Shawn got off the plane and ran like the wind to the parking lot. He had Imani in the baby carrier, little Isaiah on his hip, and Shawnee, his future pro-baller, running alongside him. His knee was killing him, but he didn't care. When they got in the car, Shawn made sure every seat belt was buckled, because he knew he was about to break some speed limits. As he flew out of the airport parking lot, he called Lily again. She still wasn't answering her phone, so he hung up and called Melvin. "Did you call Detective Jones?"

"I did. He said he would go check things out at Lily's house, but I'm not sure whether he's going straight over there or not. He didn't seem to think that Lily had anything to worry about from Jules."

"Does that mean they've already picked up Jules for questioning?"

"They couldn't find her."

Shawn wanted to throw his phone out the window. What was going on? How could the police just let Paris's killer roam free? "Thanks, Melvin. I'm on my way to Lily's house, so I'll see what's up."

⁓

Isaiah and Joel had been in the prayer room for hours. Ramona had left to go get Erin something to eat, but the two men were determined to pray until God turned this thing around.

"Lord, in the book of Malachi, You said that if I pay my tithes, you would open up the windows of heaven and pour out a blessing that I wouldn't have room enough to receive," Joel prayed. "Well, Lord, my family not only pays their tithes, but we are givers. We've done what You asked of us, ten times over, and now we ask that You pour out a blessing for us. We don't need a financial blessing, because You've already blessed us with more money than we could spend in a lifetime. What we need right now is Your blessing of protection, in the name of Jesus. Help Lily, Lord. I don't know what she's going through right now, but I feel in my heart that she is in danger. We need You, Lord, because our money can't help us out of this jam. We're depending on You."

⁓

"So, you think that Shawn doesn't want you because he's still in love with me?" Lily was getting desperate. This woman didn't seem to hear anything she was saying.

"I know that's the reason he doesn't want me. He told me so himself." The woman had started poking holes in the leather chair with the knife.

"Well, what if he falls in love with someone else after I'm gone? Are you going to kill the next woman, too?"

"I'll do what I have to do." The woman shrugged. "And besides, it not about who Shawn loves. It's about women like you and that

Paris Holmes taking men who don't belong to you. Men who were perfectly happy until you and your kind got your hooks into them."

Yes, Lily would freely admit that from the first time she'd laid eyes on Shawn Morrison, she had schemed to get him to fall just as much in love with her as she was with him. But she hadn't been trying to hurt anyone else in the process of getting her man. And this woman was a year too late on getting Lily to pay for her transgressions, because she had been redeemed. This woman needed to take up her grievance with God. "I'm not the same person who went after Shawn all those years ago," Lily blurted out. "God has changed me. He's made me a better person."

The woman gave a bitter laugh. "So, now even God loves you, huh? Is that what you're telling me?"

Uh-oh. Was God's love another sore subject for this woman? Lily wanted to live; she wanted to see her sons again. But she was running out of things to say in order to plead her case. *God, I need Your help,* she silently prayed.

Just then, there was a knock at the front door. "Ms. Washington, are you in there? It's Detective Jones."

Lily opened her mouth to yell, but the woman held the knife in her face. "You better not say one word."

But Lily felt that Detective Jones showing up at her doorstep was some kind of divine intervention. She couldn't take the chance that the detective would just leave, believing that no one was home. "I'm in here!"

The woman lunged for Lily.

⁓

Shawn brought the car to a stop several doors down from Lily's, trying to tamp down his nerves at the sight of so many police cars parked up and down the street.

"Why there all these police cars, Daddy?" Shawnee asked.

"I don't know, Son, but I'm going to find out. Do you trust me?"

Shawnee nodded.

"Then please wait here with your brother and Imani. I'll be back as soon as I find out what's going on." Thankfully, Imani was sleeping soundly in her car seat. Shawn engaged the child lock and secured the car, then started for the house.

Police officers were everywhere. Detective Jones stood at the front of the line, shouting through a bullhorn. "You might as well come out, Jules; we have the house surrounded."

Mrs. Davis, the neighbor who watched the kids for Lily when she had errands to run, was standing in the street with her housecoat on, walking from officer to officer, asking questions. Shawn asked her if she would mind getting his kids out of the car and taking them to her house.

Her eyes were frantic with worry. "Of course I'll take care of them babies. But you get Lily out of this mess. I don't know what's going on in there, but it can't be good."

"I'm going to get her out, if it's the last thing I do," Shawn assured the woman. He handed her his car keys, then turned and headed straight for Detective Jones.

⌒

"God loves you, too," Lily told the woman, whose name she now knew was Jules. The two of them lay on the floor, both clutching the knife that Jules wanted to carve her up with. After Lily had called out to Detective Jones, and Jules had lunged at her, the women had engaged in a battle that had left them panting and worn out, but neither one was giving up.

"That's not true. God doesn't love me."

"God loves everyone, Jules. Don't you get it? He loved me, even when I was running around doing things that other people found distasteful." *Like stealing Shawn from you*, Lily wanted to say, but she was too tired to keep the fight going.

At that remark, Jules seemed to loosen her hold on the knife a bit. "How did you know that God loved you, even when He shouldn't have?"

Lord, please open this woman's heart to receive the truth. "Because, no matter what I did, God kept stretching out His arms to me. He was right there, just waiting for me to repent and turn back to Him. But the thing about it was, I didn't feel His love until I was ready to receive it. Are you ready, Jules?"

⌒

"I'm going in there to get her," Shawn told Detective Jones, then started toward the house.

Jones grabbed his arm. "This isn't the football field, Shawn. You're not in control here. Now, I'm trying to get Lily out of there alive. Do you really want to do something that will hinder that?"

Shawn snatched his arm away. "I've got to do something. Don't you get it? Jules has already killed my daughter's mother. But this right here?" Shawn pointed to Lily's door. "Jules might as well kill me, if she's going to take Lily out. Because I'm as good as dead anyway."

"And who's going to take care of your sons and your daughter if you and Lily both get yourselves killed today?"

Shawn had no answer for that, but he reached for the bullhorn in Jones's hand. "At least let me tell Lily that I'm here."

Jones handed him the bullhorn.

Shawn turned toward the house and held the bullhorn to his mouth. "Lily? Lily, Baby, I'm here. And I'm not going anywhere until you come out. I need you to come back to me, Baby. Please stay strong."

⌒

"See?" Jules spat at Shawn's endearing words. "Everybody loves you. I just don't know why nobody wants to love me." Then she began to cry.

To Lily, the sound of Shawn's voice was like cool water in the middle of a desert. She couldn't hide from the truth anymore. "Yes, he loves me," she affirmed. "And you know what? I love him right back. Isn't that the kind of relationship you want? You don't really want to be with someone you love who doesn't love you back, right?"

Tears were streaming down Jules's cheeks. She let go of the knife and put her hands over her face, her body shaking as she sobbed. "All I ever wanted was for somebody to love me."

Lily picked up the knife in one hand and started rubbing Jules's back with the other. "I know somebody who will love you back, Jules. I'm going to ask you again: Are you ready to receive God's love?"

⌒

"Please don't hurt Lily, Jules," Shawn said through the bullhorn. "Let her go and take me instead. Lily shouldn't have to pay for what I did to you. Do you hear me, Jules? It was me who rejected you, not Lily."

Detective Jones reached for the bullhorn. "That's enough. We don't want to say too much."

Shawn released the bullhorn and took off toward Lily's door. Jones had said this wasn't a football field, but Shawn ran across the yard as if he was trying to win the Super Bowl.

The detective ran after him. "Don't do this, man."

"I don't have a choice." Shawn grabbed the railing and was about to take a flying leap up the steps when the door swung open.

Lily calmly walked out of the door with her arm around Jules's shoulders. Jones pulled Shawn out of the way, dashed up the steps, grabbed hold of Jules, and slapped a pair of handcuffs on her.

"Wait," Lily said, then gave Jules a hug. "Whatever happens, always remember that from this day forth, God loves you, and He has redeemed you from your past."

Shawn wanted to yell at Lily—to tell her to get away from Jules and stop trying to save the world. But he'd had his own share of redemption lately. And now that God had kept Lily alive, Shawn knew that he could no longer fight against Him. He, too, wanted God to forgive all of his sins, so he got on his knees—even his bad one—in front of Lily and everyone else standing outside, and asked God to come into his heart and forgive him of his sins.

Lily put her hand over her mouth and started crying. "Thank You, Lord; thank You," she muttered, over and over.

Shawn stood up and pulled her close to him. "What do you think, Lily? Can God redeem you to me?"

She smiled up at him through her tears. "Baby, He already has."

Shawn's cell phone rang. He looked at the caller ID and saw that it was Isaiah. "Hey, Bro."

"Hey, yourself. How's Lily?"

"She's safe, and I know you were praying, because the whole thing ended miraculously. And I think I might even be able to convince her to marry me." Shawn turned to Lily for her response.

She nodded. "Yeah, Baby, I'll marry you."

"Did you hear that?" Shawn yelled into the phone. "I am now the most blessed man on earth."

Epilogue

At the ripe old age of ninety-two, Joel Morrison went home to be with his Lord. His children and grandchildren stood around his bed as he made his departure for heaven. Joel was smiling because he had finished his work on earth. His children had learned the true meaning of giving. And, having so learned, they now could appreciate the greatest gift that God has freely given to all mankind—to all who receive His Son Jesus Christ.

No one could beat God at giving. Joel knew in his heart that the 500 million dollars that his children had given away was nothing compared to the gift that God had given each one of them—the gift of eternal life.

At the reading of his will, the Morrison children discovered that their father had about 97 million of his massive fortune left. The five children would each receive an equal share. As they left the executor's office, Shawn asked Dee Dee what she was going to do with her 19 million dollars. "Well, after I give ten percent to my church, I think I'll put another ten or twenty percent into my foundation," Dee Dee said. "But I have no clue who I want to give the rest of it to."

All five of the Morrison children burst out laughing. Because, as the executor had been telling them how blessed they were to be sharing in a 97-million-dollar fortune, each of them had been trying to figure out how he or she would bless someone else. Their father had taught them well; Eric, Isaiah, Dee Dee, Shawn, and Elaine all knew that they had been blessed to be a blessing to others.

And that is why, for years and years to come, anyone passing by Joel Morrison's massive tombstone had to stop and read the inscription: "Here lies a giver—a man who was blessed and highly favored of God."

About the Author

Vanessa Miller of Dayton, Ohio, is a best-selling author, playwright, and motivational speaker. Her stage productions include *Get You Some Business, Don't Turn Your Back on God*, and *Can't You Hear Them Crying*. Vanessa is currently in the process of writing stage productions from her novels in the Rain series.

Vanessa has been writing since she was a young child. When she wasn't writing poetry, short stories, stage plays, and novels, reading great books consumed her free time. However, it wasn't until she committed her life to the Lord in 1994 that she realized all gifts and anointing come from God. She then set out to write redemption stories that glorified God.

The Preacher, the Politician, and the Playboy follows *Heirs of Rebellion* in Morrison Family Secrets, Vanessa's second series to be published by Whitaker House. Her first series with the publishing house was Second Chance at Love, of which the first book, *Yesterday's Promise*, was number one on the Black Christian Book Club national best-sellers list in April 2010. It was followed by *A Love for Tomorrow* and *A Promise of Forever Love*. In addition, Vanessa has published two other series, Forsaken and Rain, as well as a stand-alone title, *Long Time Coming*. Her books have received positive reviews, won Best Christian Fiction Awards, and topped best-sellers lists, including *Essence*. Vanessa is the recipient of numerous awards, including the Best Christian Fiction Mahogany Award 2003 and the Red Rose Award for Excellence in Christian Fiction 2004, and she was nominated for the NAACP Image Award (Christian Fiction) 2004.

Vanessa is a dedicated Christian and devoted mother. She graduated from Capital University in Columbus, Ohio, with a degree in organizational communication. In 2007, Vanessa was ordained by her church as an exhorter. Vanessa believes this was the right position for her because God has called her to exhort readers and to help them rediscover their places with the Lord.